SHIPMENT 1

Courted by the Cowboy by Sasha Summers
A Valentine for the Cowboy by Rebecca Winters
The Maverick's Bridal Bargain by Christy Jeffries
A Baby for the Deputy by Cathy McDavid
Safe in the Lawman's Arms by Patricia Johns
The Rancher and the Baby by Marie Ferrarella

SHIPMENT 2

Cowboy Doctor by Rebecca Winters
Rodeo Rancher by Mary Sullivan
The Cowboy Takes a Wife by Trish Milburn
A Baby for the Sheriff by Mary Leo
The Kentucky Cowboy's Baby by Heidi Hormel
Her Cowboy Lawman by Pamela Britton

SHIPMENT 3

A Texas Soldier's Family by Cathy Gillen Thacker
A Baby on His Doorstep by Roz Denny Fox
The Rancher's Surprise Baby by Trish Milburn
A Cowboy to Call Daddy by Sasha Summers
Made for the Rancher by Rebecca Winters
The Rancher's Baby Proposal by Barbara White Daille
The Cowboy and the Baby by Marie Ferrarella

SHIPMENT 4

Her Stubborn Cowboy by Patricia Johns
Texas Lullaby by Tina Leonard
The Texan's Little Secret by Barbara White Daille
The Texan's Surprise Son by Cathy McDavid
It Happened One Wedding Night by Karen Rose Smith
The Cowboy's Convenient Bride by Donna Alward

SHIPMENT 5

The Baby and the Cowboy SEAL by Laura Marie Altom
The Bull Rider's Cowgirl by April Arrington
Having the Cowboy's Baby by Judy Duarte
The Reluctant Texas Rancher by Cathy Gillen Thacker
A Baby on the Ranch by Marie Ferrarella
When the Cowboy Said "I Do" by Crystal Green

SHIPMENT 6

Aidan: Loyal Cowboy by Cathy McDavid
The Hard-to-Get Cowboy by Crystal Green
A Maverick to (Re)Marry by Christine Rimmer
The Maverick's Baby-in-Waiting by Melissa Senate
Unmasking the Maverick by Teresa Southwick
The Maverick's Christmas to Remember by Christy Jeffries

SHIPMENT 7

The Maverick Fakes a Bride! by Christine Rimmer
The Maverick's Bride-to-Order by Stella Bagwell
The Maverick's Return by Marie Ferrarella
The Maverick's Snowbound Christmas by Karen Rose Smith
The Maverick & the Manhattanite by Leanne Banks
A Maverick under the Mistletoe by Brenda Harlen
The Maverick's Christmas Baby by Victoria Pade

SHIPMENT 8

A Maverick and a Half by Marie Ferrarella
The More Mavericks, the Merrier! by Brenda Harlen
From Maverick to Daddy by Teresa Southwick
A Very Maverick Christmas by Rachel Lee
The Texan's Christmas by Tanya Michaels
The Cowboy SEAL's Christmas Baby by Laura Marie Altom

RODEO RANCHER

Mary Sullivan

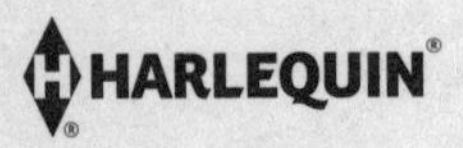

ISBN-13: 978-1-335-52321-1

Rodeo Rancher
First published in 2017. This edition published in 2022.

For questions and comments about the quality of this book, please contact us at CustomerService@Harlequin.com.

Harlequin Enterprises ULC
22 Adelaide St. West, 41st Floor
Toronto, Ontario M5H 4E3, Canada
www.Harlequin.com

Printed in U.S.A.

Award-winning author **Mary Sullivan** realized her love for romance novels when her mother insisted she read a romance. After years of creative pursuits, she discovered she was destined to write heartfelt stories of love, family and happily-ever-after.

Her first book, *No Ordinary Cowboy*, was a finalist for the Romance Writers of America's prestigious Golden Heart® Award in 2005. Since then, Mary has garnered awards, accolades and glowing reviews.

Mary indulges her passion for puzzles, cooking and meeting new people in her hometown of Toronto. Follow her on Facebook, Facebook.com/marysullivanauthor, and her website, marysullivanbooks.com, to learn more about her and the small towns she creates.

To my lovely daughter,
who inspires me every day,
and who makes me a better person.

Chapter 1

The pounding on the front door of Michael Moreno's ranch house cut through the shrieking howl of a snowstorm that had paralyzed Montana.

"Who do you think it is, Dad?" His son, Mick, didn't scare easily, but they'd all startled at the knock. Michael squeezed his arm to reassure him as the family sat together in the living room.

They spent most of their days alone. Guests were rare.

Michael frowned. "No idea. Someone in trouble, I guess." No one he could think of would venture out today.

He didn't worry about trouble. Why would he?

Nothing much bad happened in Rodeo, Montana. He lived in as safe a place as he could want for his children.

Michael shifted his daughter, Lily, from his lap and plopped her onto the sofa beside Mick. "You two stay put."

"Kiss, Daddy." Lily had taken to wanting kisses before he left the house, or even just a room.

He touched her soft cheek with his lips and dropped the book he'd been reading to them onto the littered coffee table.

In the hallway, he pulled open the heavy oak door. The noise of the wind increased tenfold, blasting him with frigid air, shocking after the warmth of the living room.

He stared at the very last thing he expected—a woman and two kids covered head-to-toe in snow.

Snow blew onto his veranda, even as deep as it was, adding an exclamation point to the first question that popped into his head. What on earth were they doing out in this storm?

"Oh, thank goodness," the woman said, stepping into the house before he invited her in, crowding him.

He stepped back.

Her bright red nose peeked out from a snow-covered pink scarf swathing her face. The kids, too, had bright red noses, and a blob of snot ran onto the little one's scarf.

"Bad day to be out," he said, his voice rife with accusation. What kind of woman took her children out in this? If she wanted to endanger herself, fine, but her kids? No.

Considering there'd been weather warnings everywhere for days, there were no excuses.

"The car broke down just up the road." She didn't seem to notice his critical tone. "I remembered seeing this light when we drove past. When I saw it I said, 'Wouldn't it be nice to be in there all toasty and warm right now?' Didn't I, boys? Then the car just went kaput suddenly, and we had to trudge all the way back. I was afraid there'd be no one here, but I figured where there's light there will be people, right? Someone *had* to be home." She prattled on, ushering her children inside, still without waiting for an invitation. The kids stopped just inside the door. "Then where would the boys and I be?"

Probably dead by morning, Michael thought, but he didn't say it. No sense frightening those two young boys. At least, he thought the woman had said they were boys.

It was hard to keep track of her ramblings, and their scarves hid their faces.

"It's absolutely frigid out there," she went on. "When we left San Francisco, it was 50 degrees. Now this. Are storms always this bad in Montana? I can't stop shivering."

"No wonder," Michael said. Seemed she didn't have the sense God gave most creatures. At least the children were decked out in snowsuits, but she wore a fashionable coat and light pants. No snowsuit. No snow pants. Flimsy fashionable boots, too—useless against a Montana snowstorm. "You aren't dressed for the weather."

She glanced down at herself. "No, I guess I'm not, am I?" Her gaiety lit up the gray corners of his house. Far as he could tell, she didn't take offense to his criticism. Strange woman. "But we were driving. We were safe in the car. I thought, 'Why would I need a snowsuit?' I bought them for the boys because they'll be playing outside once we get settled into our new home, but I won't be, will I? Playing outside, that is."

She shook herself, sending snow flying.

"Boys," she said. "Come in properly, will you? We need to get this door closed so we don't lose all of this man's lovely heat."

This man's lovely heat? Say what?

"I thought we were going to end up as human Popsicles. Oh, it's lovely in here. Mmm. Your house is so warm," she blathered on.

He'd never really understood the meaning of the word *blather*. He got it now.

"It's like an oasis in the desert," she said. "I mean, a port in the storm. Oh, you know what I mean."

She could probably teach courses in chattering. College level.

"Boys, move along so the nice man can close the door."

"Mom," the older boy said, "he didn't invite us inside. You just walked in without waiting."

The woman's bright blue eyes widened. That was saying something. They were already big to start with. "You're right, Jason. I did just walk in. You don't mind, do you?" she asked Michael, but went on before he could respond. "Of course you don't mind. We're strangers stranded in a storm. I heard people in Montana are welcoming. We can't go anywhere else right now, can we? But don't worry. We're nice people. I've taught my boys to pick up after themselves. They even put down the toilet seat when they're finished."

She noticed his children's toys cluttering

the hallway. "Your wife will be pleased with them."

Your wife. Lillian. The kick to his gut left Michael reeling. It was always bad, but at this time of year, it was—

His mind slammed shut. He couldn't think about it. Two years might be a long time to other people, but to him it felt like only yesterday that she'd…left.

He couldn't even say the word.

Died. She died, Moreno.

The littlest boy coughed.

Michael glanced at them still standing in the open doorway, noses getting redder by the second. "Come in," he said, impressed with their manners even if their mother didn't have any.

Once they were all the way inside, he closed the door, shutting out the violence of the storm.

"See?" the woman said. "I told you we'd be all right. Travis wouldn't have moved anywhere that wasn't safe for us. We are in Montana, right? The GPS on my phone stopped working yesterday. We're supposed to reach Rodeo tonight. I guess that's not going to happen."

"Rodeo? If you came here from San Francisco, you drove right past it. You didn't see the turnoff?"

She shook her head. Her shoulders seemed to slump. "We were so close." Looking around the hallway, she seemed a little lost. "The storm's huge. I barely managed to make it this far."

"This ranch is on the far side of Rodeo, about ten miles out." Hang on—she'd mentioned Travis. "Do you mean Travis Read? The new guy in town?"

She perked right up. "Yes! Do you know my brother?"

Michael had heard of him, only good stuff. Salt of the earth. Good addition to the town. Hardworking and quiet. Not at all like this ditzy woman.

Before he could respond, he got caught up in watching her unwind her scarf. She took off her wool hat and Michael stopped breathing.

She was that beautiful. Hair like spun gold. Eyes as blue as photographs he'd seen of the sea around Greece. Flawless, tanned skin.

Any man would lose his senses.

Not him, though. He was immune. He didn't think about women these days. Didn't pay them much attention. He had other things on his mind, like surviving each day.

Michael felt her older son watching him, probably gauging his reaction. At maybe nine or ten years old, and mature enough to understand the way men checked out his mom, the boy watched Michael with a knowing look. He'd seen it all before, a shame in one so young, but no wonder. What a woman.

The wind screeched. Something thumped against the side of the house. As he'd noted a few moments ago, Michael had other things on his mind, like how to get through the coming night…and what he was supposed to do with the family stranded on his doorstep.

His unexpected company might be stuck here for days. This beautiful woman might be in his house for a while.

Images of Lillian flashed through his mind, with her average looks, but more beautiful to him than any model or movie star.

The woman had been prattling again, but he'd missed every word.

She stopped and stared at the wall behind him. "Is that—is that a *wagon wheel*? On the *wall*?"

"Yeah. I'm a rancher." *You got a problem with that?* he wanted to add, but good manners held him back. He amended the thought and asked, "You okay with it?"

"Yes, of course," she said too quickly.

"What's that?" She pointed to the antique wood hand plane on the table in the front hallway.

Michael loved old tools, the ones men had used to craft and shape wood before power tools were invented. He loved the way they felt in his hand.

"It's a plane," he said.

The smaller of the boys, four or five at a guess, stepped close to the table and touched it with one finger. "That's not a plane, mister. Where's its wings?"

Michael smiled. Cute kid. "Not that kind of plane."

The boy sneezed, stirring the dust on the table.

Michael frowned. There'd been a time when his tools would have been spotless.

The woman patted her pockets and started rummaging through the bag she carried. She looked up at him, kind of helplessly. "I don't believe I have a tissue."

"I got it." Michael had wiped more noses in the past two winters than he cared to count.

He took a clean handkerchief from his pocket, wrapped his fingers around the back of the boy's head and cleaned his nose.

"Hey!" The boy tried to pull away and pointed toward the living room.

Used to children resisting handkerchiefs, Michael finished the job.

The kid struggled to peer around his legs. “There’s kids here!”

Michael turned. Mick and Lily stood in the doorway, Mick holding his little sister’s hand. Their curiosity must have kicked in when they heard all the voices.

“You can take off your coats and things in the back room.” Michael bent to help the younger boy when he struggled with his zipper. “We’ll make introductions when you’re done.”

To Mick, he said, “Show them where to put their things, then bring them to the living room.”

To the boys, he said, “Take off your boots here and carry them through.”

The little one sat down and took off his boots, nearly hauling his socks off with them.

The woman bent over to pull up his socks, but teetered on her fancy high-heeled boots.

Again Michael said, “I got it,” and squatted to pull the boy’s socks back up. They were too big for him. Must be his older brother’s.

Mick led the boys to the back of the house. When the small one ran out of one of his socks, Lily picked it up and chased after him.

While the woman—he really should get

her name soon—studied her surroundings, Michael studied her. Her tight-fitting leather jacket outlined a fairly perfect body. Long legs fit snugly into her jeans. He thought they might be what they called skinny jeans, because there wasn't much that was generous about the fit.

Women around here didn't dress like that.

A slight frown furrowed her brow.

Michael followed her gaze and found himself eyeing his home critically. Sure, he'd decorated with the tools of his trade, like the wagon wheel, but he found it homey.

All of it was real, used at one time or another over the years. Not a speck of it had been bought from a store.

This woman, with her fancy clothes, obviously found it wanting. She probably thought he was some kind of hick.

Well, he was, wasn't he?

He'd lived on this ranch just outside Rodeo, Montana, for every one of his forty years. He was a country boy through and through.

Too bad if that made him deficient in her eyes. He was who he was. A rancher. A cowboy. A man who loved horses, cattle, the land and, above all, his children.

Worse than her judgment of his decor was

the unspoken criticism of his housekeeping skills.

Bewildered, he saw his home clearly for the first time in a long while. Toys and books and some of the children's clothes littered every surface, including the carpet.

When had it gotten so bad? He used to be on top of the chores, but lately he was barely keeping up.

He scarcely managed to keep body and soul together, let alone tidying up and dusting.

Besides, he was dog-tired when he fell into bed every night. He'd been up since four thirty this morning and had put in a good three hours of work before this woman even opened her eyes.

She glanced at the carpet that obviously needed vacuuming. On the side tables, his ranching magazines hadn't even had a chance to get dog-eared, still waiting for his attention months after they'd been delivered.

On the windowsills, plants languished, every leaf caked in a layer of dust, watered only when he remembered to do it every couple of weeks.

She didn't say anything, but he felt her censure. Or maybe not. Maybe it was his own guilt.

Good manners compelled him to rise above his resentment.

"Give me your jacket. I'll hang it up."

She shrugged out of it, revealing a cardigan not even close to warm enough for the weather.

He usually associated that button-up style with old women, but there wasn't a darned thing old about her.

He kept his eyes firmly on her face and not on her spectacular—

God Almighty. His unwanted response to her beauty angered him. He lashed out with, "Leather won't keep a person warm in this weather."

At his hard tone, she shot him an indignant look. "It's pleather."

Huh? What the hell was pleather?

"I would never wear leather. Those poor animals."

Oh, Lord, a hippie-dippie animal lover.

"Do you eat meat?" he asked, working off a hunch.

"Nope."

"Figures," he murmured, and hung up her jacket on a hook to dry.

He was a rancher. He raised cattle. He ate meat. He used cattle hide in his clothing and his furniture. As long as the animal was being butchered for food, they might as well use as much of the carcass as possible.

He used glue, too, and gelatin, and whatever else was useful.

Still shivering, the woman stepped closer to the fireplace to warm her hands.

Yep. She had a fine figure, a tiny waist with shapely hips. A perfect body to match her perfect face.

Lillian could never have won a beauty pageant, but she had possessed a plain, simple beauty of her own. She wore sensible clothes in snowstorms and thought their home was comfortable and welcoming.

The visitor turned to face him, presenting her back to the fire. She held out her hand. "I'm Samantha Read."

Her long-fingered, slim hand, the fingertips still almost frozen, had a soft palm. Her grip, though, was surprisingly strong. Decisive, even. He'd assumed it would be as feminine as she looked and as flighty as she talked.

"Michael Moreno."

"Have you met my brother, Travis?" she asked.

"No, ma'am, I haven't had the opportunity."

She laughed, a cheerful tinkle. *Tinkle*? Where had that ridiculous word come from?

"*Ma'am* makes me sound ancient." Her smile knocked him off-kilter. "It's Samantha, or Sammy, whichever you prefer."

What he would prefer was that the distraction, the sheer breathtaking magnificence of her, not be in his home, and that surprised him. He wasn't easily swayed.

He kept his wide size-eleven feet firmly planted on the ground. Big feet for a man only five ten, but then all of him was wide—shoulders, chest, hands. Not to mention, a good head on his shoulders.

His unusual coffee table caught her eye. "Is that a door?"

"Yes, ma'am. Solid oak. My daddy found it on the side of the road where someone was renovating a house. Folks didn't know what they were throwing away." He was proud of his father's ingenuity. "He scraped off about ten coats of paint. Sanded for hours. Did the whole thing by hand. Gave it to me as a wedding present."

"Hmmm, interesting," was her only response.

Obviously his furniture didn't meet her high standards any more than his wall decorations did.

He'd held his rage in check throughout Lillian's struggle with cancer and her subsequent death two years ago. He'd held back his anger that his children would grow up motherless. He'd survived hell, and now this woman waltzed into his *home* and dared to disapprove.

He lashed out. "What were you doing on the road in this kind of weather? A rational person would get to the nearest motel and hunker down for the duration. You like putting your kids at risk?"

For a few moments, she stared at him with those big blue eyes. For a moment, he was afraid she'd cry.

Her expression changed, hardening, and she slowly put her hands on her hips. Her full lips thinned.

"I do everything in my power to keep my children safe."

He took satisfaction in her anger. If he had to be uncomfortable because of anger and disapproval, why shouldn't she?

She had a perfect face and a perfect body; she had probably also led the perfect life. They'd come from San Francisco. She should have stayed in sunny California if she didn't know how to handle Montana weather.

"Safe? Including driving them into a blizzard in a vehicle that wasn't trustworthy?"

She gasped. "It *is* trustworthy. It's brand-new! I don't know why it stopped. Maybe it's a lemon."

"Those kids," he said, pointing in the direction of the back of the house, "depend on you to—"

"Dad?" Mick said behind him, cutting him off. "Are you okay?"

Michael stilled at his son's anxious tone. All four children crowded the entrance to the living room. Mick and Lily stared at him. No wonder. He didn't yell. He didn't fight, especially not with strangers.

He'd done a stellar job of holding in his emotions since Lillian's death, but here this woman—Samantha—was breaking through his barriers just by being beautiful.

He wasn't even attracted to her, not really, but he knew she was attractive. A fine distinction, yeah, but he was hanging on to it with both hands.

Since when did looks ever matter to him? Especially enough to anger him?

Since his life had been turned upside down when he was barely fifteen. Ancient history. So why was it rearing its ugly head now?

Whatever the cause, he shouldn't have let the children hear him criticize her.

He cracked his knuckles. "Sorry," he murmured, knowing it was inadequate. He didn't have much more to offer.

He glanced at the kids and realized only Mick was watching him. Lily was gaping at Samantha with openmouthed amazement.

And why not?

They didn't often have visitors and rarely women, except for Karen, who was nothing like this woman with her skinny pants and *pleather* jacket.

Lily still stared. At only four years old, Lily barely remembered her mother. He kept a photograph of Lillian beside his daughter's bed to remind her.

He guessed Lily would miss her mother's touch most and, as much as he held and cuddled Lily all the time to try to fill that void, he could never *be* Lillian.

The walls crowded in on him. His breathing became shallow enough to concern him. He wasn't up to this fathering *and* mothering of them, of being both parents to them 24/7.

Samantha Read made him feel every single deficiency he tried to ignore.

He wished to holy hell she hadn't shown up on his doorstep.

Chapter 2

Samantha watched Michael come to grips with his emotions. She had to do the same with her own.

He didn't talk much, but when he did, he packed a punch.

Her hands shook. How dare he? How *dare* he criticize the way she raised her children?

Since the day Jason had been born nine years ago, her life had been all about him. Then another gift, Colt, had come along five years ago and she'd doubled her efforts.

This man didn't want them here.

Probably because of her talking. She knew she talked too much, but couldn't control herself when she was nervous.

And she had been *so* nervous when they'd been caught in the storm.

Maybe that's why his disdain hit hard.

Had she put her sons at risk? She didn't know about snowstorms. She had little experience with this kind of weather.

"I didn't know the storm was going to be so bad." She glanced out the window, baffled by the savagery on the other side of the glass. "I've never been in a snowstorm before. I had no idea what to expect."

Compelled to be honest, she added, "I should have stopped sooner, but we were so close to Rodeo. I thought we could make it to Travis's house. I didn't really know where else to stop once the storm started. I didn't see a motel."

"It got bad *really* fast, mister," Jason said.

Jason. Her defender. She wished he didn't have to take on that role. She'd told him many times not to, but still he looked out for her.

"It was just a few flakes of snow and we liked it." Jason looked nervous taking on the big stern man, but he swallowed and continued. "Colt's never seen snow in his whole entire life. Then, all of sudden, we couldn't see anything except too much snow."

"I was scared," Colt piped up.

The man's expression softened. He unbent

enough to tell Jason and Colt, "I bet you were. I would have been, too."

Ever the peacemaker, Jason said, "Don't blame my mom. It came out of nowhere. She was brave."

The man straightened and looked at her with a trace of chagrin.

Good. He should be ashamed. He was lucky she wasn't one to hold a grudge.

Maybe she shouldn't let him off the hook too quickly. She had the suspicion he felt worse that her children had heard him than he did about criticizing her in the first place.

He could fault her all he wanted. She didn't care. She knew she was a damned fine mother.

She loved her children.

What was his problem, anyway?

He watched her steadily with eyes that were deep brown, almost black, and inscrutable.

Defiantly, she gave the same kind of direct scrutiny right back.

Not much taller than her own five eight, he made up for any lack of height with an impressively broad chest and developed biceps and thighs. Dark chocolate hair curled over his collar, matching his eyes.

She might have found him attractive if he

didn't grind his hard jaw, as though *softness* and *compromise* were dirty words.

Good God, just what she needed. She'd been exposed to enough inflexible men in her line of work. She'd left all of that behind. She didn't need it here in Rodeo.

She glanced at her boys. They would make the best new start here that she could manage, even if it killed her. Her boys deserved no less.

In a month, she would start work at her new job in town and would work her butt off to be independent from everyone, even her brother.

She glanced back at the hard-edged rancher.

Maybe they shouldn't have stopped here.

Dumb thought. They'd had no choice. If she hadn't stopped, her children would have been dead by morning. This had been the only light visible through the storm.

Sammy would never admit it to the boys, but she'd been terrified.

Everyone stared at her. No one seemed to know what to do next.

The silence stretched, unnerving her. Her antsy inner neurotic raised her unwelcome head, just like clockwork. Sammy rushed to fill the space and stillness of the room…as she always did.

"Well, hey, you. What are your names?"

She leaned forward to inspect the two cute little darlings, especially the girl, who stared at her as if she had two heads. You'd think she'd never seen a woman before.

Sammy loved children. Adored them.

"I'm Mick," the boy said, his voice too loud in the quiet room. Was he overcompensating like her with her silly chatter? She guessed him to be about Colt's age. He pointed to his sister, who peeked around him. "She's Lily."

Lily was maybe three or four. A beautiful child, her mass of unruly hair, dark chocolate like her father's but shot through with red highlights, overwhelmed her delicate heart-shaped face.

"I'm so happy to meet you both. You've met my boys."

To Michael, who watched her as though she were an exotic and not-too-welcome bird, she said, "My older son is Jason, and this little troublemaker is Colt."

"Mo-om," Colt complained, but smiled as she'd known he would.

"Is it real?" Lily asked.

Sammy returned her attention to the girl. "Is what real?"

"Your hair," she whispered, clutching a doll to her chest by its mass of tangled hair.

Sammy laughed and squatted on her heels,

beckoning to her. "You tell me. Does it feel real?"

Lily approached shyly and patted Sammy's hair, then jerked her hand away as though stung.

"What? Is it bad? I'll bet it's a real mess. We've been on the road for days." She was babbling again because Michael stared a hole through her. Cripes, she was just trying to make his daughter comfortable.

"It's soft." Lily put a couple of fingers into her mouth and spoke around them. "Pretty."

"You think so? Winter static is *not* a woman's friend." She fingered the neckline of her sweater. "Watch this!"

Pulling the neck of her sweater up over the side of her head, she rubbed her hair with it.

She heard the rancher gasp. Oh, dear. What had she done wrong now? It was all good fun.

When she pulled her sweater back down, her hair stood on end on that side of her head. Her blond, almost white, hair was fine. Unless she used a lot of product, it tended to be wayward. In this dry Montana cold, it just wanted to float everywhere.

She hadn't bothered styling it lately. They were on the road driving to Travis's. Who on earth did she need to impress with perfect hair and makeup? No one.

In Vegas, she'd had to dress to the nines to impress her boss and his clientele. Not here.

Lily dissolved into the sweetest bundle of giggles, and Sammy laughed with her.

"Not so pretty now, is it?"

"No!" the child shouted, her straight little baby teeth gleaming.

She ran to her father, dragging her doll by the hair, and raised her arms to be picked up. He lifted her as though she weighed a couple of ounces. Lily whispered in his ear.

"Good, honey," he murmured back.

Whatever she'd said mellowed him. A bit. Sammy liked the way he held his daughter.

"We need to get you settled in." He glanced out the window. "You won't be going anywhere for a while."

"Dad, where are they going to sleep?" Mick asked.

His father sighed and seemed to weigh options.

"We have a spare bedroom," he said, "Trouble is I've been using it to store junk and overflow. Sometimes, the kids play in there to keep the living room clear of toys."

Samantha waited, not sure where this was going. Did he want them all to sleep on the sofa? That would be fine.

After coming to a decision, he said, "How

about all of you take my bedroom? It has a king-size bed, so there's room for everyone."

Sammy had to be sure she was putting out this family as little as possible. Jason had been right to call her to task for barging into the house without invitation. She had an impulsive nature she seemed to spend most of her life curbing.

"I couldn't possibly put you out of your room." She cast her gaze about wildly. "How about if the boys share the sofa and I can camp out on the floor?"

"No. The three of you will take my bedroom."

"But where will you sleep?"

"There's a spare bed in Lily's room."

Lily popped her fingers out of her mouth. "Daddy, no! You snore."

"It's not that bad."

Lily nodded so hard her hair flopped about. "Is bad, Daddy."

He chewed on his lip. "I guess I could put all of you in Mick's room and he could bunk with me in mine."

"No, Dad!" Mick yelled. "Sometimes I can hear you even from my room. I won't be able to sleep!"

His cheeks turned red. "If I wake you up, I'll come out here to the sofa."

"Da-a-ad. No." Mick looked miserable.

Clearly frustrated, Michael said, "Back to the original plan. You'll all take my bed. I'll sleep on the sofa."

"I can't let you sleep on the sofa while I take your bed." It just didn't sit right with Samantha.

"You sure like to argue."

"I do not!"

A smile kicked up the corners of his lips. Okay, so maybe he had a sense of humor.

"Thank you," she conceded. "We would appreciate it."

The girl whispered something in her father's ear.

"Lily wants to know," he said, "if she can show you her bedroom."

Samantha felt herself light up like a birthday cake. She loved her boys fiercely, but she had always wanted a little girl. "I'd love that."

In Lily's room, Sammy managed to keep her distance from Michael. Despite his rough-edged, stoic manner, she found him attractive.

Of all of the men who'd made passes at her in hotels, motels and gas stations on the drive out here, why did she have to feel a frisson of desire for this grumpy old man?

Old was maybe unfair. He wasn't much

over forty, but he seemed older, as though he'd started to give up.

The mauve bedroom had twin beds, both covered with duvets in shades of pink and ivory. Someone had decorated the girl's room with love. Only one of the beds was made, and it was covered with piles of clothing.

"It's all clean," the rancher said when he noticed her studying the clothes. "I leave it there after it's washed for Lily to pull out what she wants."

He sounded defensive. Maybe he thought she was judging him.

Samantha had noted how messy the place was. Maybe she *was* judging. If so, she needed to back off. She didn't know a thing about this man's life.

There didn't seem to be a woman here. Where was Lily's mother? He hadn't said anything when she'd mentioned his wife, but the man had *not* looked happy.

Something had happened.

None of your business, Sammy. Keep your concerns and your opinions to yourself.

If his wife wasn't here, Samantha suspected the guy was probably run off his feet managing this ranch and taking care of two children.

As a way to thank him for letting them

stay, she said, "I can put it all away if Lily will show me where it belongs."

He frowned at her use of the word *belongs*, as though she'd been criticizing him. She hadn't, but she could see how she might have appeared to. She was going to have to walk on eggshells with him.

"Here." Lily patted the unmade bed against the near wall. "I sleep here."

"Thank you, Lily. I figured you did. You would drown—" she gestured to the clothing "—in this stuff."

She tickled Lily's tummy and the child giggled. Lily turned to her father and wrapped her arms around his leg. So shy. Maybe she wasn't used to getting a lot of attention.

Lily lifted the scruffy doll by the hair and said, "This is Puff." She hugged her close.

Puff was an untidy, poor-looking doll, but Samantha oohed and aahed over her.

Michael smiled, but it looked grim. Samantha couldn't get a grip on who he was.

"Boys," she said, "go get your knapsacks and take them to Michael's room."

He gestured down the hallway. "Back here."

Jason and Colt returned with their knapsacks and dropped them where Mick told them.

"This is Dad's bed," Mick said a little too

loudly. He looked like a small version of his father, with adorable dark eyes framed with long lashes and brown hair curling over his collar and onto his forehead.

The boys tossed their bags onto the bed without concern. For them, a bed was a bed was a bed. For Samantha, it was different. This was the rancher's bed. She didn't know him, probably wouldn't be here long, and yet the intimacy of using his bed felt strange.

When he said, "I'll get fresh sheets," she breathed a sigh. Yes. That would make her feel better, help cut through this surreal sense of intimacy.

"Come see my room," Mick yelled to the boys and they ran out.

"Mick," Michael started, but the boys were already gone. "Sorry. Mick doesn't moderate his voice level very well."

"He yells a lot," Lily said.

She followed her father to a cupboard down the hallway. They returned with clean sheets, pillowcases and pillows.

Samantha helped Michael strip the bed even though he told her not to. She needed to help. Now that she was here, she realized how much she was putting him out.

Michael shook the clean fitted sheet over

the bed just as Lily threw herself onto the mattress. It fluttered down on top of her.

"Lily—" he started, but Samantha cut him off with a smile and wave of her hand.

She smoothed the sheet over the girl and said, "Mr. Moreno, I appreciate that you're letting us use your bed, but we can't possibly sleep here. There's a terrible lump!"

A tiny giggle emerged from beneath the sheet.

"Help! It moves," Samantha squealed. "Your bed has a moving bump!"

Lily giggled a bit more.

"It's a beautiful big bed," Samantha went on, "but I'll squish this wriggling bump flat if I lie on top of it."

Lily giggled loudly now.

Samantha laughed and looked up at Michael to share the joke, only to see a look of pain cross his face.

What was he thinking? What had Samantha set in motion with her joke?

She didn't like sadness, hated what it brought up in her. She couldn't get away from it quickly enough.

Grasping at any distraction, she picked up Lily and set her on the floor. "We'd better get this bed made."

She and Michael finished making the bed and lined the headboard with three pillows.

Michael carried his pillow and an extra quilt to the sofa in the living room.

Samantha dropped her purse onto the bed. It was all she'd brought in with her. Her suitcase had been too heavy to drag through the snow.

She joined the boys in Mick's room. He had bunk beds and a spare single bed across the room. It was a lot of sleeping space.

"This is a great room for having sleepovers. Do you do it often?"

She felt Michael's presence behind her in the doorway.

Mick looked past her toward his dad. He wrinkled his small brow. Another lock of hair fell onto his forehead. "Dad, have I had friends for sleepovers?"

"No." The single word was as curt as his tone, effectively cutting off the conversation.

What had she been thinking? Mick was still small, quite young for sleepovers. She kept making mistakes here left, right and center. Though why else would he have so many beds in his room?

Michael reached for something on the blue bedside table. "C'mere, Mick. You forgot again."

"Aw, Dad, do I hafta?"

"What do you think?"

Mick pouted but stood still while his father fitted what looked like hearing aids into his ears.

"How's the level? Good?"

Mick nodded and said, "You guys want to see the playroom?"

They all ran out of the room with little Lily trailing behind, still dragging her unfortunate doll by the hair.

Sammy stared after them.

Once she was alone in the room with Michael, the silence stretched. Strange, she could usually talk to anyone, but this taciturn man intimidated her with his silence.

She rushed to fill it. "How old are your children?"

"Mick is five and Lily's four. Yours?"

"Jason is nine." He nodded as though he'd already figured that out. "Colt is five."

Silence fell.

"Mick has hearing issues?"

"Yeah. It's why he yells. He forgets to put his aids in every morning unless I remind him. He doesn't like them. He's just being stubborn, I think."

She nodded.

The silence between them stretched. Sammy's inner neurotic raised her head again. *No. Nope. Not saying anything this time.* When she rushed to fill the void, she ended up saying the most inane things. People tended to take her less seriously than they should because of it.

Words clogged her throat, begging to be released.

"Why do the rooms have so many beds if they don't have friends over?"

"We—*I* thought maybe they'd want to someday. It just hasn't happened yet."

We? He and the children's mother?

She tried to gloss over the awkwardness of the moment. "Maybe after they start school."

"Maybe," Michael said, and changed the subject.

"We'd better take a look at the food situation," he said.

Oh, yes, food. "We're putting you out a lot, aren't we? I'll make sure the boys don't eat too much."

He waved a hand. "I have plenty of food in the freezer."

"Why?" she blurted before realizing it was an impertinent question. She tended to shop for fresh food every day.

"This is the third bad storm in two months. Meteorologists predicted a bad winter this year, and they were right. I like to be prepared."

He left the room and headed for the kitchen. She followed, interested in what he might have. She'd sensed his disapproval of her vegetarianism.

"Earlier in the week when I heard we were likely to be snowed in again, I put in an extra supply of stores. Wasn't expecting company, though."

Her hackles rose. "I'm sorry. If I could have stopped at a motel I would have."

"I'm not complaining about *that*," he said, as though there were other things he wanted to protest.

Like what?

He opened the refrigerator. "Come here and check everything out. What will your boys eat?"

"Anything."

He looked at her skeptically. "Really?"

"Just about." She studied the contents of the fridge's shelves lined with ground beef, chicken and steaks. "You've got a lot of meat."

She opened the crisper to find only root vegetables. Not a single salad green in sight.

"No greens?"

"Nope." He sounded defiant. "I don't eat 'em and the kids don't want 'em."

A loud bang at the back of the house startled her. Michael rushed down the hallway and opened a sturdy-looking exterior door. The storm door was banging against the wall of the house.

Michael latched it firmly and closed the door again. The gust of frigid air that had rushed in like an invader brought home to Samantha just how lucky she and the boys were to have found this refuge.

Grumpy guy or not, Michael had taken in three extra people who would need to be fed. It would behoove her to keep a generous heart and an open mind.

Mick stepped out of the bedroom where the children played. "Sorry, Dad, I guess I didn't hook it properly when I came in this morning."

Michael rubbed his son's hair. "It's all right. No harm done."

When he returned to the kitchen, Samantha said, "Thank you."

He pulled up short and looked behind him. Maybe he thought she was talking about closing the back door?

"I mean for taking us in," she clarified. "For letting us stay here when you don't want us here."

When he opened his mouth to protest, she

said, “It’s okay. I understand. We’re strangers. We’re an unexpected burden. When this is all over, I’ll make it up to you.”

She didn’t have a clue how. What on earth did she have to offer a man who seemed to have everything while she would spend the next few years fighting for control of her own life?

Chapter 3

Michael felt a distinct unease wash through him, a sense of shame that she knew he didn't want her here.

He'd been raised to be hospitable, to share whatever he could. Had he become such a loner that he no longer knew how to extend a helping hand to someone in need?

Well, if he had, so what?

The naked truth was that he *didn't* like strangers in his home.

He needed his solitude and his isolation. He didn't want this violation of the safe distance he'd established between himself and everyone else.

He wasn't mean-spirited or stingy. He was

just hurting and his pain was nobody else's business.

He couldn't say that, though, could he?

Even as rusty as he was with etiquette, he knew he couldn't just come right out and say, "I wish your car had never broken down near my home."

He would do whatever he had to do to make them comfortable for the night, and then he would wish them well and go back to his quiet, unadorned life.

The lights he'd turned on earlier to dispel the gloom flickered.

The woman—Samantha—glanced around nervously. He'd rather just think of her as *the woman*. Giving her a name was too dangerous in the forced intimacy of the storm.

He would think of her as Samantha because he had to, but never the more familiar Sammy she'd offered.

"Does the power go out when it storms like this?" she asked.

"Usually. I've got systems in place. I have a generator that'll kick in if we lose power, but I'll use it conservatively."

She tilted her head. "Why?"

"It runs on diesel, and we've been put on rations because of the last two storms. Gas stations were overwhelmed yesterday with everyone getting ready for this one to hit today."

"There isn't enough diesel around?"

"The county's been cleaned out this winter. It's been a bad one. Hence, the rationing."

Samantha looked nervous. "What happens when it runs out completely? What if your generator stops working?"

"We go back to the way things used to be done. I have firewood. If the furnace cuts out, the house will stay warm for a while. Once it cools down, we can all bunk in the living room on air mattresses with quilts. We can cook with camping equipment. We're good."

He didn't usually talk so much—he'd just made a speech, for God's sake—but she seemed to need reassurance.

She relaxed fractionally. "Would you mind if I use your phone? Mine stopped working a while ago. Travis thinks we're arriving tomorrow. I was pushing hard to get here today to surprise him. I need to let him know we're close but safe."

"Sure." He pointed into the living room. "At the far end of the couch."

He left the room while she made her call.

Samantha dialed Travis's number. When he answered, an out-of-proportion rush of relief left her dizzy. She hadn't realized how much she needed to see her brother.

"Sammy!" he said, and his voice was so familiar and so dear her eyes filled with tears. After all, they had only each other. Their parents were gone and they didn't have anyone else, not even the usual aunts, uncles and cousins.

"Where are you?" Travis asked. He sounded concerned.

"I made a mistake and missed the turnoff for Rodeo."

"When?"

"About an hour ago."

"*What?* You're out in this weather?"

Cripes. Was she the only one who didn't know snowstorms got this bad? She and Travis had been raised in southern Arizona, and she'd lived in Nevada for years and then California for the past year. She'd seen snow a handful of times in her life, but never a storm.

"I'm not out in it now," she replied. "The car broke down."

"But you just bought it before you left."

"I know."

"You didn't buy used, did you?"

"No! It's brand-spanking-new. I don't know what happened. It just stopped running and the boys and I were stuck."

"Stuck? Are you still in the car?" His voice had risen.

"No. We walked to a rancher's house."

"Whose house? What rancher?" Her older brother was fiercely protective of her and her sons.

"Michael Moreno."

"Hold on." She heard Travis talking to someone else. A second later he came back on the phone. "Okay. Apparently Michael's a good guy."

"That's my impression." A good guy, even if he was grumpy.

Travis sounded calmer, as though whoever he'd just spoken to had done a good job of reassuring him. "You can trust him."

She sort of, kind of already did, even though he was *obviously* not at all happy to have them. Her instincts about people were pretty good.

"We're going to stay here tonight," she said. "At least for tonight. This storm system is massive."

"I had no idea. I usually check the forecast on my phone, but it's been acting up." Unease raced through her. Now that she'd heard Travis's voice, all she wanted was to be with him. "Honestly, Travis, I didn't know what I was heading into."

She cupped the phone and her mouth with her hand so Michael wouldn't hear her. "I was so scared, Travis. I will *never* drive in a snowstorm again."

"This is a bad one. You and the boys stay put until this whole thing passes and I can come get you, okay?"

"Okay." She exhaled. She would be able to relax soon. All of the trouble of the past two years would be over once they made it to Travis's house. "Who's there with you? Your new girlfriend?"

"Rachel. Yeah. I can't wait for you two to meet. I love her, Sammy. She's the one."

"Oh, Travis. I'm so happy for you." She was. Truly. "I've wanted this for a long time."

It was just strange for Travis to have someone. Not just a girlfriend, but *the one*. He'd never talked about love before though he'd had plenty of girlfriends, even that phony Vivian he'd been so infatuated with. Thank God that hadn't lasted.

But who was this Rachel? How had he fallen so hard so quickly? What was she like? Could Sammy trust her to love Travis as much as he deserved to be loved?

"I'm going to marry her, Sammy."

Samantha choked. When she stopped coughing, she whispered, "Marry?"

"Yep." Her brother had never sounded more certain.

"I'm happy for you, bro." She was, but a tiny part of her knew that this changed everything.

She bit her lip. "Where will you live? In the house?"

"Yes, with her two children."

Rachel had children? "But—" She'd thought the house would be a home for her and the boys.

"It will all work out, Sammy. We'll make it work. You're going to love Rachel and her girls," Travis said, and his calm confidence soothed her even while she still worried. How on earth was it all supposed to work?

Sammy and her boys would never again have her brother's undivided love and attention.

Well, wasn't that the point you were going to make when you arrived at the house he bought for you? Weren't you determined to pay him every cent he paid for that house, even if it took years?

Weren't you the one who was going to finally fight for independence from every single man, even your brother?

Her father and her ex-husband had let her

down. Depending on men sucked. Only Travis had been trustworthy.

"I love you, bro."

"And I love you, sis. Tell the boys I love them, too."

"I will. Bye." She hated to hang up, hated to wait another day or two before seeing him, before moving to a happier home than this one seemed to be. But the house she was moving to with Travis would soon contain another woman and two more children.

She just didn't know what to think.

Everything was topsy-turvy. Her ex had taught her some hard lessons about life. She would find a way to be independent, for her own sake and her sons'.

If the house didn't work out, she would find some other place to live. After all, she was a hard worker and had a job to start next month.

Turning away, she found Michael watching her. "Is everything okay?" he asked. "Did you get through?"

She smiled. "Yes. It was good to talk to him. Thank you."

"How long has it been since you've seen him?"

"Close to six months." She rubbed her hands on her thighs and shivered.

He frowned. "I didn't ask. Did your clothes get wet in the snow?"

"My pants are really damp."

"Follow me." He led her into his bedroom. "I'm a lot wider than you, but we can find something."

He handed her a pair of gray sweatpants. "You can cinch these with the string at the waist. If that's not enough, I'll find you a belt."

He also gave her a sweatshirt, which was faded but soft. "Layer this over your sweater to keep warm."

Michael left the room. The pants were snug in the hips, but big in the waist. She managed to tie the string tightly enough to hold them up. She put on the sweatshirt and immediately felt warmer.

In the bathroom, she hung her pants over the shower stall to dry.

She joined him in the kitchen. "Thanks. That feels a lot better." She stepped close to the counter. "We should probably start cooking, right?"

Damn. Samantha looked good in his clothes. They weren't the least bit feminine, but she made them so…and that was a problem.

Michael turned away from her to open the

fridge door, resisting even the faintest hint of awareness.

"We do need to cook," he finally said in answer to her question. *Lighten up, Moreno.*

He might not be able to control the situation, but he could control his reaction to it. "It's better to have the food cooked before we lose power. It'll keep longer than raw."

"What's all the meat for?"

"Chicken soup and meat loaf. The kids like both."

"My boys would like that, too."

So they weren't vegetarians like her? Strange.

He got the proteins out of the fridge.

"That's a lot of ground beef," she said.

"I was going to make a couple of loaves. I'm not much of a cook, but I can handle the basics."

"Would you mind if I check your cupboards to see what else there is?"

He spread one arm wide. "Have at it."

He stood back, leaned against the doorjamb and crossed his arms while he waited.

He didn't like having her in his kitchen, but maybe she could come up with more ideas to feed six people with his supplies.

She dived into the task, surprising him with

what excited her. A tin of black beans nearly sent her into raptures. He almost smiled.

"You have spaghetti and canned tomato sauce. Your spices look old, but we can try to jazz it up a bit. How about one meat loaf and a pot of Bolognese?"

"We're having bologna?" Mick asked. He stood behind Michael with the other children.

Samantha spun around. "Bolognese. Basically, beef sauce for spaghetti."

Why didn't she just say so? Awkward and unsophisticated beside her with her fancy words for meat sauce, he bristled.

"We're hungry," Mick said.

"You keep checking out the food," Michael told Samantha. "I'll make snacks." He gave them cheese strings and granola bars.

"They need a fruit or veggie with that."

He knew how to feed children, for God's sake. He had two of them. The woman didn't seem to notice that she'd butted in. She insisted they have apple slices spread with peanut butter. Health freak.

Not a bad idea, though. They carried their snacks to Mick's bedroom.

She rummaged through his cupboards again.

"Barley!" she squealed.

"You get excited about strange things," he said.

"I can use it to make a vegetarian soup for myself."

He cocked his head. "You said your sons eat anything. Aren't they vegetarians, too?"

"No. I've told them my philosophy, but they can eat what they want and make their own choices when they're old enough. They eat all of my food, but if anyone offers meat, they eat that, too."

Hell of a way to go about it. He taught his children his values and he expected them to follow. He didn't give them choices.

He shrugged and moved on. No skin off his nose if she was a screwball parent.

"What are you comfortable making?" he asked.

"I love cooking soups. Do you want to make the meat loaf with half the ground beef and brown the rest for the spaghetti sauce?"

"Suits me fine."

While he focused on the meat, she started pulling out every vegetable in his crisper—cabbage, carrots and celery.

"Do you have potatoes?"

"I'll get them. How many do you want?"

"As many as you have."

"I've got ten pounds."

While she digested that, she chewed her bottom lip. "An entire bag?"

"Close to it."

"There are six of us. Should we use half of them to make mashed potatoes to go with the meat loaf and bake the rest?"

"Yeah. We can always eat them cold tomorrow if need be."

He stored the bag at the top of the stairs to the basement. He retrieved it and also snagged a rutabaga and a bag of onions.

He returned to the kitchen and came up short. It was strange to see a woman there and even stranger that he had to pass close to her to get to his own counter.

Careful not to touch her, he sidled past, feeling her heat nonetheless.

It was going to be a long night.

She asked, "Are you sure you'll have enough food? We're three extra mouths."

Without a word, he opened the freezer door. Loaves of bread filled half of the space, with plenty of meat crowding the other.

"Living this far from town, I'm always prepared."

"Hey!" she declared, reaching in as though she'd found a treasure. "Look at all of this spinach. Awesome! You said the kids didn't eat greens."

"For some weird reason, Mick likes the frozen stuff, so I keep plenty on hand."

"May I use it?"

"Of course."

They worked side by side for an eternity, or so it seemed to Michael. Every time he had to pass her to get into the fridge, or to retrieve a pot from a low cupboard, he held his breath.

She was almost as tall as him, maybe only a couple of inches shorter. He wasn't used to that. Lillian had been a little bit of a thing.

The first time they brushed arms, he just about jumped out of his skin.

He wasn't the skittish type, not usually. He might not be attracted to this woman, despite her beauty, but he also wasn't used to having a woman in his kitchen. Other than Lillian's friend Karen, that is, who came around more often than he liked under the guise of helping him with the children.

Things were getting complicated there. All Michael felt for Karen was a small level of affection. He'd known for a while now that she was expecting more from him than he wanted to give.

She'd been good to him, and he felt nothing other than gratitude. It made him feel ashamed…and guilty.

Samantha brushed past him again. He

glanced her way sharply, but she wasn't doing it on purpose. The working area of the kitchen was just too damn small for two people who didn't know each other.

The harvest table took up pretty much all of the room, but at least there would be plenty of space to seat everyone at dinnertime.

Earlier, when she'd pulled her sweater up over her hair for Lily's benefit, she'd revealed a trim waist and perfectly tanned tight flesh. His libido had performed a tap dance worthy of Gene Kelly.

It had been two and a half years since he'd been with a woman. Once Lillian had become too weak for intimacy, all he'd done was hold her.

Maybe sometime in the two years since her death he should have slept with a woman. But who? This was a small town. Everyone knew everyone else and all of their business.

He suspected the town might already think he and Karen were having relations, even though he'd been careful to set boundaries there.

Did his physical discomfort matter? In the space of a silly heartbeat, Samantha had won over his daughter. That had been clear when Lily had whispered, for his ears only after that trick with her hair, "I like her, Daddy."

That was good enough for him, even if he did find her ditzy and too beautiful.

She puzzled him. Without a speck of self-consciousness, she'd messed up her own hair, just to break the ice with Lily.

In his experience, beautiful women cared too much about their appearances. His mother had. So had his baby sister.

Michael strengthened his defenses and set his confusion aside. The power could go out at any time and there was a lot to do.

Between the two of them, they managed to make the meat loaf and put together one pot of chicken soup and another of spaghetti sauce.

Samantha had made a small pot of barley soup for herself and had used the steak to make a larger one of beef and barley.

Michael had also boiled and mashed potatoes—more potatoes than he'd seen in one place since he was a child with his mom, dad and Angela around.

"Oh," Samantha breathed, breaking into his thoughts of the past. Good thing. He didn't want to go there.

"I just had a thought," she said.

"What?"

"If the power goes out and we have to conserve diesel, how will we heat this up? How will we cook the pasta?"

"Camping equipment on the fireplace. I have a kerosene camp stove I can use on the back porch as well as a barbecue I can cook just about anything on."

Samantha looked curious and engaged, as though the details truly interested her. "How about if I make things easier by boiling the spaghetti now and mixing it with the sauce? Then we can reheat in one pot."

Opening the door of the refrigerator, she said, "I saw some Monterey Jack in here. I can add cheese to the pot to make it tasty."

"Sure. Lily will like that. She loves that cheese."

She stopped what she was doing and became pensive. Seemed out of character for the woman. "Oh. It's Lily's cheese. Okay, let's leave it for her."

She put it back into the fridge almost reverently.

"She won't mind if you use it," Michael insisted.

Her smile looked a little sad. "I'd like it to be hers."

Weird. What was wrong with the woman? Lily wasn't going to die if she couldn't have a piece of cheese.

She seemed adamant, so Michael reached past her for the cheese, calling, "Lily, come here."

Samantha's perfume floated around him like a soft cloud. He held his breath, grabbed the cheese and backed away from her.

Lily ran into the kitchen, cheeks flushed. "What, Daddy? Hurry. I have to play."

"Your Monterey Jack cheese. You okay if we use it in some spaghetti sauce or should we leave it for you to eat?"

"S'ghetti sauce!" She turned and ran to the back of the house.

"You have permission. Use it," he ordered, dropping it into Samantha's hands.

"Okay."

"You like children? Especially girls?"

Her lips twisted, her smile rueful. "Oh, I do. I really do. I wish I'd had one. Don't get me wrong," she rushed on. "I love my boys to heaven and back. I wouldn't trade them for *anything*. They are my heart. I do like little girls, though. I guess I just relate to them."

What had that sadness been about with the cheese and Lily? Somehow he didn't think she would have reacted in the same way had it been Mick's cheese.

He didn't want that kind of curiosity about

her. The less he knew about the woman, the better.

Samantha started to chatter about everything and nothing and he wondered what the heck was going on. Something had made her nervous.

When she paused for a breath of air, he said, “You going to quit talking any time soon?”

She caught her breath and stared at him.

He hadn’t meant to sound harsh. It was meant to be a joke. He might not want her here, but he didn’t willingly hurt others. He was about to open his mouth to apologize when she burst out laughing.

“Travis says that *exact* same thing to me all the time. He says I’m long on air and short on content.”

Her smile, like sunshine bursting through heavy clouds, turned his guts to pudding.

Chapter 4

Abruptly, Michael turned away, jittery and resisting this woman with all his might.

He didn't even *know* Samantha. She was a stranger and yet she was turning him inside out.

"I need to put that living room together. Who knows how much more time we have? Better to do it now than when we lose power. With the strength of this storm, we'll lose it for sure." Now he was the one babbling.

"Put the room together? What do you mean?"

"I'll blow up air mattresses and haul out all of our quilts and extra bedding. We might be sleeping in front of the fire tonight."

"May I ask you to do something first? Or I can do it."

She was doing enough already. Her industriousness surprised him.

Why? What had he expected? That because she was beautiful, she'd be spoiled and temperamental? Well, yeah. That had been his experience.

He stopped and turned to face her.

"What is it?" he asked, wary.

"Can you vacuum before you put all of that on the floor?"

So she didn't like his housekeeping. Michael stiffened. Tough.

Samantha placed slim fingers on his forearm. At her soft touch, he stiffened further and she dropped her hand.

"I don't mean to criticize. It's just that Jason has asthma. He's growing out of it, but it still affects him. I don't want to risk an attack when we're stuck so far out here."

Out here in the back of beyond, she means, he thought bitterly.

She must have guessed what he was thinking because she clarified, "In this storm it would take forever to get him to the hospital. It's terrifying when he can't breathe."

"Fair enough." He dropped what he was doing and got out the vacuum cleaner. Where a child's health was concerned, he didn't take chances.

In the living room, he started to pick up all of the children's toys, but she interrupted him.

"Can we do something else first?"

He stilled, wary again. "What?"

"Follow me."

Going into Lily's room, she picked up an empty laundry basket.

"Children," she hollered like a drill sergeant, startling him. The woman had a healthy set of lungs. "We need you in the living room."

They ran after her. In front of the fireplace, she plopped the basket onto the floor.

"You see all of these toys, books and clothes?"

They nodded.

"They all—every single last one—are going into this basket. Who do you think is going to pick them up?"

Colt emitted a long-suffering sigh. Michael watched Samantha bite her cheek so she wouldn't laugh. Her kids knew her well.

"Us?" Colt asked.

"Yep," she affirmed. "But there will be a reward."

She turned to Michael.

"Do you have any cookies?"

He nodded. "A box of Oreos."

Samantha clapped her hands. "Good! When you're finished picking up everything, Michael will carry the basket to the back room and you'll each get a couple of cookies."

The kids jumped to the task.

Michael turned to her with one brow raised. "Bribery?"

"Works every time." She grinned and returned to the kitchen.

All right. Again, fair. She'd gotten the kids to clean the room to allow him to vacuum for her boy.

Michael carried the full basket to the playroom, returned with another basket that they also filled, and gave the children their cookies.

He went back to the living room to vacuum.

While he did that, another new scent emanated from the kitchen. It smelled like biscuits baking in the oven. His stomach grumbled.

Samantha made a couple of dozen biscuits that came out as light and airy as any Michael had ever tasted, including Vy's at the Summertime Diner in town, and that was really saying something.

For dinner, she insisted that they have a second vegetable with the meat loaf along with potatoes. She heated frozen corn in the microwave. She also added some to her bean-and-barley soup.

Michael called the children to the table.

"This is a huge table," she said, running her hand along the oak grain.

"It's a farm kitchen. Used to be the ranch hands ate in here with us."

"Ranch hands? Where are they?"

"Slow time of year. Any who wanted to were allowed to go home for a month of holidays. The rest opted to ride out the storm in town. Violet at the Summertime Diner will find a way to cook meals even without power. They'll be a lot tastier than mine." His laugh sounded rusty.

Lily and Mick took their usual spots at the table. Michael directed Jason and Colt to the other seats on either side of the table and offered Samantha the one at the other end.

"You have your choice of food." He outlined the menu for the kids.

"Can I have a little bit of everything?" Jason asked. "I want meat loaf, but I really like Mom's soups."

"In this house, you can have whatever you want and as much of it as you can shovel into your faces."

The younger children giggled. Jason took him seriously.

It turned out Samantha's children ate a lot. She seemed embarrassed by it. Maybe because of his less-than-gracious welcome when they arrived? He didn't like that their appetites bothered her, but at least she didn't stop them from eating.

After dinner, they got out his air mattresses and inflated them. Jason manned the electric pump while Michael carted in wood and lined the walls beside the fireplace.

He sent Samantha to the linen closet for sheets and plenty of blankets. She made up the two double air mattresses into beds and added extra blankets to Michael's quilt on the sofa just in case.

Michael built up a fire so there would be warm ashes in the grate if the power went out overnight.

Jason followed him to the basement to retrieve his camping equipment. He was a good kid, helpful and uncomplaining. Samantha had done all right with him.

They carried up his old pots and pans. Battered, they'd seen a lot of campfires and had stood in during power outages many times over the years.

He took out his battery-operated emergency lamps.

Fascinated by all of it, Jason asked question after question about how things were done around the house during a snowstorm.

"What about your animals? You have cows and horses, right?"

"The horses and some of my cattle are safe in my barn and stable. The rest are in pens around the property. I went out first thing this morning and gave them plenty of food and water to get them through the night."

Arms loaded, they mounted the stairs to the main floor. Michael closed and locked the door behind him to keep the younger children out. "In the morning, if weather permits, I'll go out and take care of them."

Excitement lit Jason's face. "Can I come?" he blurted, and then looked contrite. "Sorry. I shouldn't have invited myself. It's just that I like animals."

"You can come," Michael said quietly. The kid's interest should be honored.

"Thanks." The boy's smile lit up his intelligent face. Michael guessed there was a lot going on under Jason's polite exterior, more than met the eye. He needed a chance to grow and develop in his own ways.

Shortly after eight, Samantha sat on the

sofa and rummaged in her big bag for something.

Lily, in Michael's arms, wriggled to be put down and went over to her. Apparently, the ice had really and truly been broken with that hair trick, because Lily leaned against Samantha's thigh to look inside. "Want to see what I'm carrying, do you?"

Samantha dumped the contents onto a sofa cushion. "There you go. I have everything in here but the kitchen sink."

At that moment, the phone rang.

Michael answered. "Hello?"

"Michael. You're there." It was Karen Enright and she sounded anxious.

Michael bit back a sigh. Karen had been Lillian's best friend. After Lillian's death, Karen had become proprietorial where Michael was concerned. Her boundless earnest concern for him and his children smothered him. He'd never given her one iota of encouragement.

"I've been worried." Her breathless voice irritated him.

The only woman he'd ever loved was dead. He wasn't about to start loving someone else. Karen should understand that.

He'd loved Lillian from the first moment

he'd met her in high school. It had deepened when they'd begun dating at sixteen.

Lightning had struck him once. It wasn't likely to strike him a second time.

"How are you and the children?" she asked. "Would you like me to come over and help take care of them?"

Her deep *earnestness* chafed him.

"In this weather? For God's sake, Karen, stay put." Honestly, he just wanted her to stop. "Like I said earlier, the kids and I will be fine."

"But what if the power goes out?"

"We'll do what we've always done. We'll get by. Do not come over. It would be a fool's errand."

Suddenly, the phone went dead and the lights went out.

They'd lost their power, just as he'd thought they would.

The living room had been plunged into darkness, save for the fire he'd been feeding before the phone rang.

Damned cordless phone. He should have stuck with his old landline.

Lily patted his leg. "Daddy? Okay?"

"Yep. We're good."

"We've got systems," Mick said. "See, Lily?

Right, Dad?" In the light of the fire, he pointed to the logs and the camping equipment.

"We'll be fine," Michael said. "In the morning, I'll start up the generator. We won't need it for the night. Might as well head to bed." Reluctant to give in to the intimacy of sleeping in the same room with strangers, he thought the bedrooms might stay warm enough until morning. He led the way down the hall with one of the lamps and tucked in his daughter and kissed his son.

Samantha did the same with her two boys and then they were alone in the hallway.

Her fingers twisted nervously.

He stuck his hands into his pockets and raised his shoulders, not sure what to do with her. It was only nine o'clock and too early for bed.

"You want a coffee or something?" he asked. "We can boil the water over the fire."

"Too much caffeine. Do you have herbal tea?"

"Think so."

They wandered to the kitchen. The urge to keep his distance from her was stronger now that the house was hushed and felt even more intimate.

She started to chatter again. He did his best to block it out. He couldn't.

"You don't have to do that," he said.

She stilled. "Do what?"

"Fill the silence."

For a moment she went deeply silent. He wondered whether he'd been too blunt. Again.

She didn't laugh this time. "It's a habit of mine."

"I noticed." He smiled to soften things in case he really had hurt her feelings.

He found the herbal tea in the cupboard, Lillian's chamomile. Toward the end it was the only thing that would settle her stomach.

Lost in memories, he didn't realize he was staring at the box, immobile until a light touch warmed his arm.

"Are you okay?"

"Yeah." He sighed. "It was my wife's tea."

"Is she—? Did she—?"

"She's gone." He hated uttering the word *dead.* Every time he did, it made it real all over again.

Samantha didn't ask questions, but said, "You don't have to give me her tea."

But he did. Lillian had been generous to everyone. She would have liked nothing better than to sit down with Samantha and talk about their kids or anything under the sun that caught her fancy.

She would have wanted Samantha to enjoy what was left of the tea now.

"Let me make you a cup. I want to."

She nodded and stepped away.

They settled in the living room, her on the sofa and Michael keeping his distance in the armchair.

He didn't know what to say.

Apparently, neither did she.

She wasn't rushing to fill the void even though her fingers moved constantly. Why was she so nervous? Sure, he was a stranger, but he thought he'd shown he was trustworthy. He wasn't going to jump her. Maybe if he told her the truth about Lillian, she wouldn't be afraid to be alone with him.

"My wife didn't leave us," he blurted. "She died."

She gasped. "I'm sorry for your loss." She looked it. "It must be hard for you and the children."

The unspoken question hung in the air until he answered it. "Cancer."

"So…not sudden."

"No. Might have been better if it had been." Okay, enough. He couldn't talk about it. It hurt. He didn't often haul out his intestines without anesthesia and put them on display.

A log popped on the fire and she startled.

"The boys' father?" he asked to change the subject. "Is he around?"

"We're divorced. Last I heard, he was in the Himalayas somewhere."

He raised his brows, but she didn't expand.

Her expressive face had gone blank. Was she angry? Sad? Glad?

"How could he leave his children behind?" He hadn't meant to say it out loud, but anger had surged through him. Lillian hadn't had a choice, but if she had, she would have stayed. It sounded like Sammy's husband had run out on her. He would be angry. He would seethe.

"That's a good question," she answered. "I've wondered that many times." Yes. There was the anger.

"Must be hard on the boys." He echoed her earlier sentiment, because it was true. All of this was difficult enough for the two of them as adults, but what were children equipped to handle?

"Yes, it has been hard. Jason felt abandoned when his dad left. He's my little protector. He thinks he needs to be the man of the family. I wish he could relax and just have fun like Colt does."

Michael nodded. He'd already noticed Jason's love for his mother. The boy had stood up to him, a big strapping adult, to defend her from implied criticism.

Gutsy kid.

"He wants to come out with me in the morning to see the animals. I said yes. That okay with you?"

She seemed to ponder the implications… a man alone with her child. She must have sensed his honesty.

She nodded. "It's hard, isn't it? Trying to keep our children safe?"

"Yeah. It is." And he didn't always get it right. Some people in town thought he kept his children too isolated, but how could he not?

What if something happened to one of them? It was his job to make sure they reached adulthood unscathed. He hadn't been able to save Lillian, but he could save his children.

Samantha awoke in the middle of the night to tapping on her forehead.

For a minute, she thought there was a drip from the ceiling, but the tapping was dry.

A hand!

She startled awake and took in a lungful of air, ready to scream. No! Not here. Not in rural Montana where she and her sons were supposed to be safe.

Prepared to protect her children, she opened her eyes.

The person hovering over her in the darkness was tiny. A child.

Sammy's disorientation cleared and she remembered where she was.

Her breath whooshed out of her. She glanced to her right. Both of her boys slept soundly. Who was patting her hair?

She mumbled, "What is it?"

"I'm cold," Lily whispered not an inch from Sammy's face.

Oh! Michael's little girl.

Sammy realized she was cold, too. The house had lost its heat pretty quickly. No wonder. The storm still raged outside.

Good thing Michael had lent her his sweat suit. She'd be chilled without the fleece.

Without further thought, she said, "Climb in. We'll cuddle together. Okay?"

Samantha snuggled Lily and spooned around her, while Colt poked his elbow into Sammy's back. Jason slept soundly on his brother's far side. Thank goodness for Michael's huge bed.

Lily backed right up against her. Sammy

pulled the blankets up snugly around all of them. She wrapped her arms around the child.

"Better? Warm enough?"

"Warm." Lily sighed and dozed off right away.

Her sweet little weight against Samantha melted a path to Sammy's heart.

"I always wanted a little girl," she murmured, and yawned.

Despite her exhaustion, sleep didn't come easily. She touched each of her boys, relieved to feel their healthy, slightly sweaty heat. It took a while for her heart to stop racing.

She didn't want to, but she thought about Manny d'Onofrio and his associates.

In his letter from jail, her former employer had promised he'd called off his men. He'd written that he no longer sought revenge against her for sending him to prison. In his words, *I found God and I want peace. I won't bother you no more for ratting me out.*

God, didn't that sound like a bad movie script? But it had been all too real for Sammy, starting with getting a job in Manny's Las Vegas casino as part of his accounting team and ending with her testifying against him for embezzling funds from his partners.

He'd vowed revenge, but she believed he'd

changed. In his letter, he'd sounded sincere. Who would have thought?

But sometimes, late at night, she worried. Nightfall brought terror.

It was over. It was all finally over. Why couldn't she stop jumping at every late-night sound?

Travis had bought the house here for her and the boys as a sanctuary, away from crooks and city crimes. Hence, her trip in a snowstorm to Rodeo.

She'd gone back to her own name, dropping her married name, and had given it to her boys, too, and no one was supposed to know where she was. Manny's letter had reached her through their lawyers. He couldn't find her, but Travis's former girlfriend, Vivian, had tracked him here.

Vivian used to work for Manny.

Manny might guess she would follow Travis here, but he'd sworn he wouldn't bother her again. Even so, she'd decided to leave the sanctuary they'd found after Las Vegas, in California, and follow Travis to the house he'd bought for her.

She could afford Rodeo a lot better than she could San Francisco.

Manny told her she was safe. She believed him. Even so, at night…

Samantha heard the logs in the fireplace being moved around. Michael was keeping the fire alive.

Strong, sturdy and dependable judging by how devoted he was to his children, Michael would protect all of them.

Sure, she planned to never depend on a man again, and yes, she would let Travis off the hook now that he had his own life sorted out. He was no longer responsible for her, as he had been ever since they were kids.

She was searching inside herself for independence, but for tonight, just for this one night, Samantha would relax into being cared for again.

The house might be cooling, but they would be safe with Michael down the hallway taking care of them.

She nodded off.

In the middle of the night, Michael awoke to a frigid house. The ranch-style abode was well-built, but a wind as strong as this seemed to seep in through the walls.

He'd been up a couple of times already to stoke the fire.

Chilled, he groped for the emergency lamp he'd left beside the sofa. Once he had light, he built up the fire yet again to warm at least this one room.

There was no way around bringing Samantha and her children to sleep in the living room. Not only had her family invaded his home, now the two families had to sleep together. Michael's world narrowed from a ranch, to a house, to a room. Too much intimacy.

Carrying the lamp down the hallway, he stopped in Mick's room and woke him. "It's getting cold. Move to the living room."

Mick grumbled, but did as he was told.

In Lily's room, Michael found the bed empty. A chill that had nothing to do with the storm shot through him.

"Lily?" he called, not caring if he woke his guests. They had to be moved anyway. He checked the bathroom. Not there.

"Lily?" he called more loudly. It wasn't that she could go anywhere—the outer doors were locked and she couldn't open them—but he didn't like not knowing where she was.

One result of losing his wife was that he panicked when he couldn't locate his children.

"In here," he heard a faint murmur.

He stepped into his bedroom. His bed was full of three kids and one woman.

Samantha opened her eyes and said, "She was cold. I hope you don't mind. I let her come into bed with us."

He didn't mind, not exactly. He liked that Lily had a loving woman to cuddle against, but this woman was a stranger, not her mother.

He fought the never-ending, pervasive anger that simmered inside him like an unwanted guest.

The children mumbled themselves awake.

"House has cooled down too much," Michael explained. "Everyone into the living room."

He handed Jason the lamp. "Light the way for us."

He scooped up his daughter.

"What's happening, Daddy?" Her weight against his chest, her hair catching on his five o'clock shadow, normalized him. He relaxed.

"We're moving in front of the fire. Remember we did it in December and January, too?"

"No."

"You were pretty young back then. You're a big girl now." It was only February.

She liked when he called her a big girl, so he did it often.

"Big girl," she whispered against his shoulder. Her head popped up. "Sammy come, too."

"I'm coming, sweetie. Brrr."

Don't get used to her, Lily. She'll be gone in a couple of days. Maximum.

Michael had come to the unwelcome realization that this woman and her children wouldn't be going anywhere tomorrow. Even if the storm abated, the roads this far out of town wouldn't be cleared immediately.

Once everyone was in the living room, an air of excitement took hold. The boys jockeyed for the best spots closest to the fire.

They settled in on the air mattresses, with Samantha and all four children on the two doubles pushed side by side.

Michael made sure the grate covered the fire securely and that none of the blankets came too close to the hearth. He took to his bed on the sofa again.

"Everyone warm enough?" he asked.

Only Samantha responded. "Toasty. I guess the children are asleep already."

Just before he turned off the flashlight, he saw his daughter cuddle as close to Samantha as she could.

To his troubled surprise, he found himself thinking, *I don't blame you.*

Chapter 5

Michael awoke, as he always did, in the predawn hours, stretching out the kinks in darkness. The world wasn't yet quiet. The maelstrom of the storm still raged, but his animals needed to be cared for again today.

Time to see how they'd fared overnight.

He unfolded himself from the heavy quilts on the sofa and built up the fire. After a little coaxing, it burst to life.

That should keep everyone warm until I get back, he thought, then turned to see how his guests and his children were doing.

Lily still lay curled against Samantha under a half dozen layers of quilts, bedspreads and duvets.

Mick had kicked off his covers, but curled into a ball, cold in his sleep, no doubt. Michael tucked the covers back around him.

He stood and stretched, only to find one pair of eyes open and studying him.

"You okay?" he asked Jason. "Warm enough?"

"Yeah," Jason replied, rubbing his eyes. "Are you going out to your animals now?"

"Yeah."

"For sure it's okay for me to come?"

Michael regretted saying he could last night. The stables and the barn were his refuge, *his* place, almost sacred to him.

He didn't go back on promises, though. "Sure, if you dress warmly enough."

Jason jumped out of bed and nearly plunged off the mattress, displacing his younger brother, who slept through it all. Michael tucked Colt in as well and led Jason to the back of the house.

"You use the toilet first before you get dressed. Don't flush. I'll go after you."

While Jason did that, Michael got dressed. Jason scurried into Michael's cold room to don his clothes and Michael used the facilities.

When he came out, he found Jason getting

into his snowsuit. Wind still howled around the house.

When they were ready, he said, "Come on, son."

He heard a quick intake of air from Jason and cursed the slip of his tongue. Obviously it was a problem for the boy, with his father unavailable overseas. He hoped the animals would take the edge off Jason's grief.

Before they stepped outside, Michael put a hand on Jason's shoulder.

"Listen, this is the way it's gotta be. It's still storming. We won't be able to see where we're going."

"Because it's dark outside?"

"No. Because of the storm. Even if it wasn't still dark, the storm would block out everything around us."

He pointed to a rope tied to the back of the house. "This runs from the house to the back door of the stable. We're going to hang on to it and let it guide us all the way there. As long as we do that, we can't get lost or disoriented. Don't let go. Okay? Not even for a second. Not even to rub your nose. Got it?"

At Michael's stern tone, the boy nodded.

"You going to be warm enough?"

"Yeah. It's cold out, but I feel fine."

"It's going to be tough getting through

this." Michael stepped down from the porch, sinking thigh-deep into snow. "Walk right behind me. I mean *right* behind me. Right in my footsteps, okay? Grab hold of the rope with one hand and the back of my coat with the other. Hold tightly."

The wind snatched the words out of his mouth, but Jason nodded.

It took them a good ten minutes to muscle across the yard to the stable.

Once there, Michael took down a couple of shovels hanging on the outside wall, beating snow off of them. Between the two of them, they cleared enough snow to open the door.

The warmth and humidity of the animals greeted them when they entered. "Let's get started on the chores."

"It's warmer in here than outside," Jason remarked, his gaze flitting everywhere, drinking it all in like a half-starved man.

"You ever been in a barn or stable before?" Michael grabbed pitchforks for each of them.

"A couple of times, sir."

"The name's Michael. You can use it."

Jason nodded, his eye on the horse in the first stall.

"This is Rascal." Michael rubbed the horse's nose.

"Is he called that because of his character?"

Michael grinned at the astute kid. "You bet. Do you know how to do any chores?"

"Yes, sir. I mean, Michael. We didn't see a lot of horses in Vegas, but my uncle Travis took me out to whatever ranch he was working on when he could."

"Vegas? I thought your mom said you drove in from California."

"Yeah. San Francisco. We only lived there a year. I grew up in Las Vegas."

Odd place to raise a family. He'd never do it, but to each his own.

Michael introduced the boy to his horses, and the kid took to them like an otter to water.

He didn't seem to mind the chores. He raked out the stalls happily, even though there was manure in among the straw.

Jason hauled fresh straw from the end of the aisle and food from the bin Michael directed him to.

Used to doing these chores day after day on his own, the boy's presence was an odd balm to his soul. Michael hadn't realized he'd been lonely, not out here, at any rate.

Sure, he missed Lillian with a fierce ache, but she hadn't come out here often. This had always been his domain, but what a joy to share this with a child who was eager and willing to learn.

So far, Mick hadn't shown a speck of interest in the animals.

They worked steadily before heading to the barn. Again, they grabbed the rope Michael had rigged.

In the barn were all the cattle he hadn't left out for the winter, the pregnant cows and the old ones he should have gotten rid of, but couldn't. He shouldn't be such a softy.

"Is this all of your cows?" Jason asked, patting the nose of a heifer who'd nuzzled his cheek.

"Nope. A lot are out in this weather. I have three hundred cows. I can't house them all."

Jason's eyes widened. "How can they stay alive outside?"

"Just like in the house, I've got systems for the land. Every fall, the ranch hands and I check the fences to make sure they're sturdy, then build up windbreaks with bales of hay."

He started clearing out soiled bedding and providing fresh.

"The cattle will huddle behind those barriers to get a break from driving wind and snow and to keep each other warm."

Jason fell in step with him, helping as well as any one of his ranch hands.

"Before the storm, I provided extra feed. It boosts their metabolism and increases body heat. Just like with people. Once the storm settles, I'll get out to check on them and provide more feed."

He brushed his hand over one of his cows. "See her shaggy coat?"

Jason nodded, soaking it all up.

"The cattle outside will have even thicker winter coats."

"What will they drink? Snow?"

"Nah. They can't take in enough like that. I go out often throughout the winter to break up the ice that covers their water tanks. It's one of my chores, but when it gets bad, I've got water heaters I turn on in the tanks. No matter the weather, there's still water available."

They worked for a couple of hours until Jason's stomach rumbled.

Michael was reluctant to go back to the house, to that living room that felt too crowded. Nonetheless he said, "Let's go back inside. We need breakfast."

They fought their way back to the house with their hands on the rope.

Inside the back door, Michael barely had time to take off his boots before he heard yelling in the living room.

Michael smelled smoke. Alarmed, he ran for the front of the house.

Smoke filled the living room. Samantha opened windows while the kids shouted at her and snow streamed inside. Mick used a ranching magazine to fan the fire.

When he saw the problem, Michael calmed down. "Here, give me that. You're making it worse."

He took the magazine from Mick and had him sit on the sofa. He ordered the other children to do the same.

Samantha came over and clutched his arm. "I don't know what I did wrong."

He shook off her hand. "The fire had burned too low. You put a log on nothing but ashes and all it did was smolder and smoke. You needed to build it back up slowly."

He didn't need this kind of mayhem. Usually when he came in from the stable and barns, the children were still asleep and he could have his first coffee of the day in peace before waking them up for breakfast.

Instead, the house was full of panicked children and one scared woman.

He used a poker to push the log to the side of the firebox.

"Here, watch for next time." *Next time.* Michael's heart sank. He couldn't get his house back to himself soon enough.

Best to concentrate on the good in the situation. He'd liked teaching Jason.

"Come here." He assumed the boy might be interested in learning this, too. Sure enough, he was.

Michael taught both mother and child how to build a fire.

Jason's interest didn't surprise him, but Samantha's did. She seemed excited, even.

"Show me how to cook breakfast on the fire," she ordered.

She leaned close.

Turning away, he asked the children what they wanted.

"Bologna sauce," Mick shouted.

Michael sighed. "Mick, where are your hearing aids?"

His son stomped to his bedroom. A minute later, he returned smiling. He had an enviable resilience. If only Michael could learn from his son.

This time when Mick said, "Bologna sauce," his volume was normal.

Colt and Lily took up a chorus of *bologna sauce* with Mick while they beat their heels against the sofa.

Samantha, Michael noticed, did not correct them.

"Bologna sauce it is," she said with a laugh. Another person who bounced back.

Cripes, he was surrounded by a bunch of beach balls while he was attached to the earth with iron shackles.

Michael set up a grate that held a pot for Samantha to fill with the cooked spaghetti and meat sauce.

Then he went to the back porch to get his barbecue utensils from the big plastic bin beside his grill.

The kids came running as he'd known they would.

"Wow," breathed Colt, staring out the back window. "Look at the snow. Everything's white. I can't even see your backyard."

When he returned to the living room, he found Samantha at the front window, looking at the road.

"We're not leaving today, are we?" she asked sounding more than a little lost.

"'Fraid not," he responded.

She turned away from the window and said quietly, "I'm sorry."

He shrugged. He didn't want them here, but he couldn't dwell on it. The kids performing hijinks in his living room needed to be fed.

"Take this." He held out a long-handled spoon.

She took it and scooped spaghetti and sauce from a big plastic tub into the pot.

She stirred it regularly. Michael had trouble keeping his distance while making coffee at the edge of the fire.

Samantha took one sip and said, “Not bad.”

“I’m surprised you like it. I would have taken you for a latte kind of gal.” He shouldn’t make assumptions, but she’d just driven in from San Francisco and those kids had grown up in Vegas.

“Hey, I’ve had espresso in some of the trendiest coffee shops out there. *Espresso.* If I can handle that, I can handle anything.”

After they’d eaten and cleaned up, they gathered at the warmest spot in the house, on the two air mattresses in front of the fire.

“I’m going to turn on the generator for a while. Do whatever needs to be done that you need electricity for. Use the toilet and flush it.” Michael stood up. “Once the house is warm enough, take showers. This afternoon we’ll rely on the fireplace again.”

Once the generator was on, they washed dishes and bodies before heading back to the air mattresses.

Samantha said, “It’s going to be a long day if these children can’t get outside.”

“That won’t happen today. It’s wicked out

there. Jason and I had to fight the wind and snow to get to the stable. We had to use the rope attached…to…the…house…"

He trailed off when he saw the anger on her face. "You put my son in danger?"

Jason heard her. "Mo-o-om, I wanted to go. I held on to the rope and Michael's jacket. He took good care of me."

When she still looked angry, Jason told her about everything they'd done with the animals and how much he'd enjoyed it. Gradually, she softened.

Michael had to turn away to hide a smile. The kid sure knew how to handle his mother…and she had no idea she'd been handled.

As he turned back, her gaze cut to him. Wrong. She knew exactly what her son was doing. She might have forgiven her son, but there was no such forgiveness for Michael.

"You said he could go."

"I didn't know it would be dangerous."

"I made sure he was safe."

She relaxed.

After lunch, she asked, "Can you leave the generator on for another hour or two? May we watch TV?"

At his raised brow, she said, "I don't usually advocate TV as a babysitter, but we're going to run out of things to do. Let's watch TV now while the house is heating up and then play other games when it's off."

Michael turned on the television, but they got only fuzz. "Let's watch a movie."

He put *Finding Nemo* into the DVD player and moved to settle into his armchair, but Samantha said, "Wait!"

Everyone stared at her.

"How can we have a movie without popcorn? I saw corn kernels in the cupboard."

Lord, this woman liked to plan and direct things to *death.* Why couldn't they just watch the movie and be done with it?

Like the pied piper, she led the children to the kitchen and returned ten minutes later with two big bowls of popcorn and drinks for everyone.

"Can we start the movie now?" The hint of sarcasm in Michael's tone slid off her back.

Queenly among her subjects, nestled in the middle of the sofa with two kids on either side of her, she nodded her head.

He pressed Play.

At the end of the movie, Michael turned off the generator.

They gathered on the air mattresses to make an early dinner over a freshly lit fire.

To the children, Samantha said, "This is

fun, isn't it? We're camping in the middle of winter."

"Camping inside is fun!" Mick and Colt jumped and brayed like donkeys.

Dinner was baked potatoes sliced and fried on a pair of cast-iron skillets over the fire and then dumped into a pot to keep warm. Michael fried slices of meat loaf and Samantha heated a bowl of soup for herself.

After dinner, with energy still coursing through their veins, the children chafed against the enforced inactivity.

"You know what this calls for, don't you?" Samantha jumped up from her seat.

"Mom, don't," Jason said, dropping his head into his hands.

Ready to intervene on the boy's behalf, Michael leaned forward until he noted the glint in Samantha's eyes.

"Don't what, honey?" she asked. "Don't sing?"

Jason lifted his head. "You can sing, but please, Mom, no—"

Samantha grinned. "No, what?"

"No disco!" Jason shouted.

His mother laughed and launched into a raucous version of "I Will Survive."

The kids cheered and jumped up to join

her, dancing around while she clapped her hands. Lily warbled, "I will surbibe."

Michael and Jason exchanged rueful glances.

Where did Samantha find the stamina? Even as her energy and life swirled around him, he resented the chaos and disorder. He wanted his quiet life back.

The performance seemed to wear out the children. When they wound down, Michael understood her strategy. Smart woman.

"Mom," Colt said. "Tell us a story."

They stretched out on the mattresses and Samantha started.

"Once upon a time, there was a pretty princess…"

"Mom," Jason said seriously. "Get real."

Samantha laughed and said, "Okay."

To Michael, Jason confided, "She does that every time and she still thinks it's funny." He said it with a smile. Kid sure did love his mother.

Samantha told a story about machines that turned into people and people who turned into machines.

"Want the princess story," Lily mumbled at one point, but the boys were fascinated.

Michael watched and listened, drawn in

despite himself. She had a gift, this woman, of turning adversity into fun.

At nine o'clock they turned in for an early night.

In the quiet after the children were asleep, her husky voice said, "We survived the day."

Michael resisted her voice and her sentiment and her allure. He resented her invitation for him to join the land of the living.

He didn't want it.

The land of the living was overrated.

He'd been just fine before she came into his house yesterday. So had his kids.

He thought of Lily running into the kitchen yesterday with color in her cheeks and excitement in her voice when she said, "Hurry, Daddy. I have to play."

Lily needed the land of the living. So did Mick.

"Yeah," he finally said. "We survived."

A long time later, Michael fell asleep in his crowded living room.

Michael got up multiple times throughout the night to stoke the fire.

Every time, Jason rolled over to ask, "Is it time?"

"Not yet. It's the middle of the night. Go

back to sleep, son," Michael said the last time. *Son*. He could have bitten his tongue.

Jason rolled over and went back to sleep.

At five, answering the call of his inner clock, Michael got up to tend to the animals. Jason joined him again.

In the mudroom, Jason said, "Something's wrong."

"Naw. Nothing's wrong. The storm's abated, that's all. There's no wind."

Jason brightened. "That's what it is. Yeah." He pumped his fist.

When they stepped outside, the crisp, quiet air brought them up short.

"You warm?" Michael asked.

"Yeah. It's cold out, but nice without the wind."

"It's a good time of day. Calm. Peaceful." Michael stepped down from the porch, sinking into thigh-deep snow. The path he'd forged yesterday was gone.

He started in on making a new path, muscling his way through.

"Walk in my footsteps, okay?"

They did their chores in silence, like a well-rehearsed team.

An hour and a half later, they entered the house to the sound of Mick and Colt kicking up a fuss.

"They're bored," Michael said. He knew from experience children didn't last long in enforced seclusion.

Michael turned the generator back on and they cooked their breakfast on the stove. The novelty of cooking over the fire had worn off.

They cleaned up after breakfast and brushed their teeth and washed up, all while Michael ignored Samantha, ruthlessly quashing the memories of her flushed face while she sang disco songs last night.

He stood stunned in the chaos of his living room, wondering how he was going to get through the rest of the day.

He needed to find something to fill the hours.

They tried playing cards and board games, but ran out of steam after an hour.

Cabin fever had set in firmly.

"What are we going to do now?" Colt asked.

"We need to get outside to play for a while," Michael said. "You kids have to burn off energy."

"Yay!" Colt ran for the back door and looked out. "Let me feel the snow."

By the time Michael realized his intentions, Cody had opened the back door, hauled off his socks and stepped right out into the snow.

"Hey!" Michael yelled. "What do you think you're doing?"

"I never felt snow before. It's cold. It's fun."

"It'll freeze your toes off." Michael hooked him like a giggling sack of potatoes under one arm.

"Mick and Jason, secure the doors. Lily, bring Colt's socks."

He set the boy on his feet in the living room. "Silly kid," he said. His smile was strained. The house had been without spirit and fun and excitement a long time, but the four walls were closing in on him.

Okay, the fun part of the strangers being here was fine. The rest, the whiff of attraction to Samantha, the unsettling urge to move, to *do*, to get away from the house and all of its too many occupants, was not. He was tired. He wanted to be left alone.

Chapter 6

All Samantha could see from the back door was a path forged through a thigh-high wall of snow.

The isolation and the close quarters were starting to wear on her. Pulling Michael out of his glumness and keeping the children happy was taking a toll.

She wanted time alone, in particular away from Michael. He was too big, too solid, too *present* for her comfort.

The silence of the nights away from city streets and the bright lights of Vegas left her antsy and wanting to turn on every lamp she could find. Impossible during a power outage, of course, and frustrating.

She wasn't willing to throw in the towel yet, though. Not by a long shot.

She'd lived through a lot in her life. She could survive this.

How on earth were the children supposed to play in snow that was almost over their heads? Especially Lily's.

Michael put his hands on his hips. "Jason, can you go to the stable and get the two shovels we used earlier to open the door?"

"Sure."

Jason stepped outside and Samantha reached to draw him back. Michael touched her arm, shaking his head.

"He's fine," he said, voice low and quiet. "He can do it."

"Don't tell me how to raise my son," she bit out.

"Then don't tell me how to raise *my* children," he shot back.

Stalemate.

He dropped his hand, and she was glad. The tingling awareness his touch generated unsettled her.

She'd managed to keep her distance from him, metaphorically at any rate. Now to keep things that way until she could leave. He made her skin feel too tight.

Jason trudged down the path he and Michael had created earlier in the day. Snow had fallen in from the sides, but he managed just fine.

Samantha turned to look at Michael. "How did you know he would be okay?"

"I was doing the same thing at his age. He's a really good kid. He seems to like helping."

"He does." She bit her bottom lip. "Sometimes I worry he does too much. He's growing up too quickly. He had to—"

Stop. Don't tell this stranger too much. He doesn't need to know more about Kevin.

Ah, hell. They were stuck together for a few more days. Michael should understand who he was dealing with.

"He had to grow up too young. His father was an absentee father even before we divorced and he left the country. At first he was proud that he'd fathered a son, but he lost interest quickly."

Michael cocked his head. "How could he lose interest in such a great kid?"

"He was self-absorbed. I didn't realize that when I married him. So Jason has grown up without a father for most of his life."

When she'd married Kevin, she'd thought her dreams of a secure family life and all of the things she'd missed in childhood had finally been answered. She'd been so wrong.

She shrugged and felt Michael studying her. Finally, she looked up at him.

"You've done a fine job. He's a great person."

High praise from such a self-contained man. Oh, high praise, indeed. She tried to resist the warmth that spread through her, but couldn't. Yeah, she'd done a *great* job with her sons. *Take that, Kevin, and put it in your hookah and smoke it wherever you are. We don't need you. We're during just fine on our own.*

When Jason returned, Michael pounded the shovels against the steps to remove snow and carried them down the hallway.

Over his shoulder, he said, "Jason or Samantha, one of you bring the shovel from the porch."

Jason snagged it before Sammy could and followed him, her son so eager to please. What if he developed hero worship for Michael?

We're leaving soon, Jason. Be careful, honey.

Jason already had a bad case of that with Travis, but that was okay. Travis would always be there for his nephews. This stranger would not.

"Come on," Samantha said, and she and

the children trooped the length of the house to the front door where the snow wasn't piled quite as high on the veranda as it had been against the back door.

They could actually stand outside.

Michael snagged another shovel from the wall and handed it to Samantha.

He dug out two child-sized plastic shovels and handed them to the boys.

"Okay, everyone shovel." To Samantha, he said, "Can you and the children clear the veranda while Jason and I shovel a path to the truck?"

She stared at the landscape, snow blue-white in the day's brilliant sunshine. "Gorgeous," she whispered.

Whiteness dappled by silvery glitter stretched across fields as far as the eye could see. Fat blobs of snow weighted the branches of trees.

Michael's garage was covered in a layer of snow that looked like it should cave in the roof.

The road beyond his property hadn't been plowed. Only the slightest mound of snow in the distance hinted at a car stuck there.

Michael moved to step off the veranda, but Samantha stopped him with a quiet question. "We're not going anywhere today, either, are we?"

"Nope," he said. He didn't sound happy. She didn't know what to do about that. She was trying to be amenable and pleasant, but something was bothering this man.

Shrugging, she turned to the children. "Shovel," she said, softening the order with a smile.

They dug in. Samantha's arms got more of a workout than they'd had in a long time.

"Whew! This is harder than lifting weights."

Michael's answering smile could only be termed a mocking tilt of his lips that said, *tell me something I don't already know.*

It irritated the hell out of her. Of course he knew all of this stuff. He'd grown up with it. She hadn't.

Michael and Jason stepped up onto the veranda. "Good," he said. "That's done. Thanks for your help."

"That's it?"

His brow creased. "What do you mean?"

"We get to shovel the snow, but we can't play in it?"

"It's too deep for the little ones."

Samantha took off her borrowed mitten and shoved wayward locks of flyaway hair back under her borrowed hat. Staring at the front yard, she tried to come up with something more the children could do. She wanted to give them at least another half hour outside.

Besides, they all had cabin fever, and this break from it hadn't been nearly long enough.

Michael made an impatient sound low in his throat.

"I'm thinking," she cracked out, then just as quickly adjusted her attitude. This family was being put out by hers. She needed to hold on to her patience. "Sorry. There must be some way to play out here."

She snapped her fingers, then pulled her big mitten back on.

"I've got it!"

The children picked up on her excitement. "What, Mom?" Colt jumped up and down.

Lily wrapped her arms around Sammy's leg and stared up at her, waiting.

Mick shouted, "You got what?"

Michael rolled his eyes. "Mick, when we get back inside, what do you have to do?"

"Put in my hearing aids?" he yelled.

"Yup."

Mick grinned.

Samantha studied Michael, glanced down at Jason and then the other two children. She blurted, "Snowball fight!"

The kids hooted, but the man scowled. "How do you plan to manage that?" He tilted his head at the thigh-deep snow.

Talk about attitude adjustments. *He* needed one.

"Listen." She stepped close to him. She knew she was being bossy, but couldn't help herself. "There are four children who *need* to be out in this snow. If we take these kids inside now, we'll still have half the day and all of tonight for them to get stir-crazy again."

Michael had the good grace to respond with, "You're right."

"The longer we stay outside the better, and the more settled they'll be later on."

He nodded reluctantly, but agreed nonetheless.

Lily patted her leg for attention. Samantha bent down. She shouldn't interfere, should just let Michael raise his children his way, but her resolve couldn't withstand those dark chocolate eyes that so matched her father's.

In Lily, she saw herself at that age.

No way, Sammy. No comparison. Her life is completely different from yours as a child. Compared to you, Lily is living like a princess.

Even so, Samantha read notes of loneliness in Lily's need to get close to her. Sammy was a stranger, but clearly the child needed something from her.

In that need, Sammy saw vestiges of her own loneliness in childhood. She did *not* want this child to be lonely.

Leave it, Sammy. None of your business. Leave it.

She couldn't.

"So, what we have to do is this," she blurted, reaching beyond her common sense, her caution and her fear of this man's reaction.

She pointed to a spot about eight feet from the house. "Can you and Jason go down the path and then cut another path across the front of the house parallel to it?" she asked Michael.

His jaw worked, as though he were chewing on something small. Clearly, this man did not like being told what to do. "Why?"

"I'm going to get the smaller children to gather up some of that snow we pushed to the ends of the veranda and pile it against the railing here at the front."

A puzzled frown marred a face that would be handsome if he weren't so grouchy.

"After we finish, we'll all make snowballs." She gestured toward the front railing. "The children will hide down here with me, behind our wall. You and Jason will hunker down in the trench you make down there."

Jason grinned. "Then we'll throw them at each other. We can't play *in* the snow, but we can still play *with* it."

She smiled broadly at her smart son. "Exactly, Jason."

Michael's face lit with subdued appreciation. "We can do that."

When he stepped onto the path to plan their trench, Jason said, "My mom always has the best playing ideas."

"This is a good one," the rancher conceded, wide in his shearling coat and cowboy hat. "Yeah. It's all right."

One grouchy cynic at a time, Samantha thought. *This is how the arguments of the world are won.*

The younger children threw themselves into the challenge just as soon as Samantha told them they were building a veranda fort.

After that was done, she sat on the bottom step with Lily and helped her to form snowballs while Mick and Colt ran down the sides of the path and made their own.

Mick had to teach Colt how to do it. "You're getting the hang of it really well, Colt," Samantha said.

"I love it, Mom. I wish we'd always lived with snow."

"You say that now," Michael said from the new pathway he was shoveling. "But just wait until you've had to shovel it a couple of dozen times a winter."

About to call him out for raining on Colt's parade, Samantha pulled herself back.

Michael's comment might be negative, but there was a nice smile in his voice.

He might be grouchy with her and deeply unhappy about the situation, but he didn't take it out on her children.

When they had a stockpile of snowballs, Samantha squatted with the younger children behind the railing.

Mick peeked around the newel post, then yelled, "Now!"

The kids and Samantha stood up and tossed snowballs at Jason and Michael, standing up in their snow trough.

Samantha took a snowball to the face. Lily, whose head barely cleared the top of the railing, laughed when Sammy spit out snow.

"Woohooo! Let's get 'em," Samantha shouted, and the children tossed volley after volley of snowballs at Jason and Michael.

Once they'd exhausted their supply, they

lay down behind the snow and giggled until Samantha's sides hurt.

She could hear Jason and Michael talking, but ignored them when Lily threw herself against her and squealed, "That was fun! I like snowball fights."

"Do you usually win or lose?" Sammy asked.

"I never had one before."

Samantha stared at her and then at Mick, who said, "Yeah. That was the first time. I loved it. Let's do it again."

Unsettled by their artless sharing—they lived with all of this snow, but had never had a snowball fight—she redirected their attention.

"It was fun, wasn't it? Sure, we can do it again, but let's eat first. I need to make lu—"

When the snowball hit the side of her head, the children burst into gales of laughter.

Samantha cleared the snow from her face and turned to find Jason smiling at her. "Gotcha, Mom."

"You sure did."

Just then, Michael reared up from behind him and grabbed Mick, throwing him into the snow in front of the veranda. He did the same with Colt.

When he picked up Lily, she started to cry.

Bewildered, he stared helplessly at the girl. "What's wrong?" he asked.

Lily buried her face against his jacket and clung to him.

"I think she was scared when you burst onto the veranda," Samantha explained quietly. "I don't think she understands it's a game."

She lightened her tone. "Lily, look at the boys!"

Lily lifted her tearstained face and looked at Mick and Colt rolling in the snow like a pair of puppies.

"They're having fun. Your daddy was playing a game." Samantha noted how Lily rubbed her eyes with her wet mittens. "Do you want Daddy to toss you into the snow, too? He'd be happy to."

"No, Sammy. Maybe amorrow."

"Okay." To Michael, she said, "Someone's *t-i-r-e-d*. We should go in for lunch."

He whispered to Lily, "You want bacon for lunch?"

Watching him now, Samantha saw a man who might be reserved and more than a little uptight, but he loved his daughter.

"Bacon, Daddy."

"Lots? A million slices?"

"A million, Daddy. And one more. 'Kay?"

"A million and one it is." He called to the boys. "Do you need help getting out of the snow?"

"Yeah! It's deep."

Michael tried to put Lily down, but she clung to him like a burr.

"Will she come to me?" Samantha reached out to her.

"Sammy!" Lily all but jumped into Samantha's arms.

After a brief flash of emotion that Samantha couldn't decipher, Michael passed the child over and stepped off the veranda to rescue the younger boys.

When he came back out of the snow with one under each arm, Samantha said, "Look, Lily, your father has two sacks of potatoes in snowsuits."

Lily giggled. "Want 'tatoes, Sammy. And bacon."

She asked a question of Michael. "Do we have a lot of bacon?"

He nodded. "Enough for everyone."

"Good. Bacon and potatoes for lunch for everyone!"

Samantha set Lily on her feet at the door.

"One more throw," Colt and Mick chanted.

Michael threw them, one after the other,

into the snow. He laughed and it was good to see. Jason went next.

Without thinking, Michael turned to pick up Samantha, holding her body hard against his. She squealed and their eyes locked.

Horrified, he dropped her. She stumbled back against the front wall of the house.

He stared while emotions roiled across his face like approaching thunderclouds. Clearly, he'd let down some wall, some defense, and had relaxed around her. Clearly, he regretted it.

So did she. He felt too good, too strong and too attractive.

Fortunately, the children missed the byplay on their way into the house.

They took off their boots and ran to the back porch to store them and to hang up their outerwear.

Rummaging in the kitchen with shaking hands, Samantha found the rest of the Monterey Jack she hadn't used for the Bolognese.

She slathered butter onto the leftover biscuits to make small sandwiches the children could munch on while the bacon cooked.

Sensing Michael's presence behind her in the kitchen doorway, she chattered, "Those children will have big appetites after all that.

They must be starving. I had a blast. I never knew snowball fights could be so much fun."

When Michael didn't respond, Samantha turned toward him slowly. When he'd picked her up to toss her into the snow, a barrier had broken.

His dark eyes watched her quietly, solemnly, with one big shoulder leaning against the doorjamb and his sturdy hands shoved into his jean pockets.

"Thank you," he said.

She glanced down at the half-buttered sandwich in her hand. "I don't mind throwing together a few sandwiches. You're welcome."

"I don't mean the food." He shifted until he stood straight. "I'm talking about playing with them. Making a special game for them." He shrugged, his expression uncomfortable. Why? At having to talk so much? Expressing thanks? Remorse at having let her in past his defenses, even if so briefly?

"Thanks for giving them fun," he said.

Heaviness, a solemnity that made her uneasy, spread through her. She started chattering again. "Goodness, don't worry about it. Your children are a lot of fun. My boys like to have fun. It was easy for me to take advantage of that."

"Stop," he ordered, and she did. On a dime.

She knew she talked too much when she was nervous.

"You did a good thing for my children and I'm thanking you. That's all."

She said, "You're welcome."

Another stalemate and another truce.

He stepped into the kitchen and cut open the two pounds of bacon. Grabbing a plate and what looked like fondue forks from a bottom drawer, he started to leave the kitchen, but stopped.

"It was all good," he said over his shoulder, then entered the living room.

Samantha carried in the frying pans and potatoes and handed them to Michael, chock-full of warm fuzzies.

Stop. For God's sake, stop. Don't fall for this man. You'll be leaving here soon and getting on with the rest of your life, taking care of yourself and your boys.

Men, except Travis, can't be trusted. Depend on yourself and no one else.

Chapter 7

Michael had hated Samantha's game.

She'd made him relax. She'd made him forget.

Well, maybe hate *is a strong word*, Michael thought, but he'd disliked her bossiness, her intrusion into his family and…how well it worked.

It was none of her business if his children had never had a snowball fight.

Okay, yeah, if he was honest, it had been fun. Even for him.

That was why he'd thanked her, for the children.

But when she and her children left, his two kids were going to really feel it.

He was a good father. He was, dammit.

He glanced at Lily asleep in Samantha's lap and cursed a blue streak to himself.

There were so many reasons why he didn't want a woman in his house he'd lost track.

The list ended with him never, ever falling in love again. Period.

If pain were sold by the bucketful he would be a millionaire. Why would he willingly put himself through heartache again?

His kids might be falling for her, but he wouldn't.

Cripes, why was he even thinking about this? She'd only turned up here two nights ago.

So why were his children so attached to her already?

Because she was fun.

Michael couldn't deny that.

Fun didn't last, though. Sooner or later, there would be trouble. There would be heartache. There would be an illness or a betrayal that would bring on the inevitable darkness. Guaranteed.

His mother and sister had taught him that lesson at the tender age of fifteen. Mom had taken thirteen-year-old Angela away. They'd left to find fame and fortune in Hollywood because Angie had been strikingly beautiful. Drop-dead gorgeous.

After Mom left, Dad sank into despair and bitterness. It eventually killed him. That and the bottle he'd turned to.

Every day, Michael ran home from school hoping for a letter from his mother, a note, a postcard, anything, but every day he went to his room disappointed while his dad drank himself into oblivion.

Why had his mother loved Angela to distraction and hadn't loved *him* at all, not even enough to send him one card in the years since she'd left? And why hadn't Angela ever tried to contact him, either?

Once he became an adult, he'd tried to find them, but they might as well have dropped off the face of the earth.

Then he'd married Lillian. He'd thought she was his happy ending, and she had been, but fate had robbed him of happiness. Again.

He couldn't stay in this living room with too many people in it.

The claustrophobia that had started after Lillian's death arose in his throat and he clawed at the collar of his sweater, pulling it away from his neck.

He couldn't breathe.

Maybe it was because he hadn't had his

mornings alone, his one spot of sanity in his day, his one chance to get away from his kids…and wasn't that an awful thought when he and Lillian had worked so long and hard to finally have their two precious children?

He jumped to his feet.

Jason and Samantha, the only two not napping in the after-lunch lull, startled.

"I need to go out for a while. Would you… ah…watch the children?"

Even as he resented her presence in his house, he'd take advantage of it to be alone.

For just a few damned minutes.

Without a partner, he was constantly at his kids' beck and call.

He loved them, even as he needed time away, even as he worried when he couldn't see them. What a mess.

Maybe he should hire a babysitter sometimes, but he couldn't. He just couldn't bring people in to handle his own children, and he couldn't let others see the depths of his ineptitude. He had never wanted this kind of life.

As hard as he tried, he was only coping. He wasn't getting ahead. And yet, he had no idea what else to do. Or how else to behave.

He had no blueprint for constructing a new, happier life for himself and his children.

He loved his children. Bottom line, his life

was about them. But was he doing enough? Why did he resent them in odd moments?

All he had were good intentions...and they weren't anywhere close to enough.

Outside the back door, he gulped cold air into his lungs, hoping against hope that it could wash away the taste of his own failure.

That woman sitting in his living room brought home to him exactly how much he was failing.

Every time she devised fun games for his children, she might as well hold a damned mirror to him to say, *Look at the man who should be doing more.*

"Are you okay?"

Michael spun around. Jason stood on the doorstep, a little scared, probably because Michael had run out of the house so abruptly.

Cripes. Couldn't he have even these few seconds alone?

The kid cared. He shouldn't. He was too young for that burden, and Michael resented the intrusion. Jason's concern smothered him.

"I'm good. Go back to your mother." His frustration leaked through in his voice.

The kid looked crestfallen. His shoulders drooped. He shrank back into the house and closed the door behind him.

Damn. How many ways could one man let those around him down?

He opened the door and called to Jason, who'd almost reached the living room.

"Come back. Get dressed. Let's go check the animals." He should have done it this morning, but instead he'd been tempted into having *fun*.

Jason brightened and turned around. Michael waited while he put on his snowsuit and boots.

Outside, they walked the path to the garage. Once there, Michael backed a snowmobile out and told Jason to hop on.

They toured the ranch, checking on cattle and feed and water.

He pointed to a water tank. "See? Water's still clear. The heaters are working."

"The cows survived, didn't they?"

"Yep. They sure did. You want to help me put out more feed?"

He felt Jason nod against his back.

They worked for the next hour making sure there was enough feed to last through the night and into tomorrow, then returned to the garage.

Jason laid a couple of shovels across his lap and they drove out to the car stranded on the side of the road and cleared it off.

"There. Now the plows won't run into it. Get your mom's suitcase out of the trunk."

When they were done, with the suitcase sitting on Jason's lap, they returned the snowmobile to the garage and left the suitcase at the back door.

In the stable, Michael led the way to the back of the aisle, stopping to talk to the horses along the way.

From against the far wall he pulled out a couple of ancient wooden sawhorses his grandfather had built. He set them up in a large square of extra space at the end of the aisle.

He lugged a couple of saddles onto them and got out old rags and polish.

He called to Jason, who was farther up the aisle petting Rascal.

Once Jason neared, Michael handed him a rag.

"You ever polished a saddle?"

"Nope."

"Sit down. I'll show you how." He pulled a couple of old wooden kitchen chairs over and they sat. He showed the boy how much polish to use, how far to spread it on the leather and how long to polish it.

They worked in harmonious silence. With

each swipe of the cloth, with each repetitive act, Michael calmed.

Despite the chill that seeped in from outside, he savored the animals' warmth and the soft shuffling of their hooves.

Animals demanded no more of a man than regular food, water and exercise.

Even the occasional flatulence from the horses didn't bother him.

The first one set Jason giggling, though, and Michael smiled. Oh, to be so young and carefree that a fart made you laugh.

"That was a stinker," Jason said.

"Some of them are."

Other than that exchange, they hadn't spoken.

The boy was quiet, didn't intrude and didn't chatter a mile a minute like his mother did.

Why?

Was he sensitive to Michael's mood? Or was it that he'd learned to be careful around grown-ups? Or had he learned to settle for less attention?

Speculation would get him nowhere, but he wouldn't intrude on Jason's privacy by asking. He sensed he was as private as Michael himself was.

His back stiffened as he chilled. At four thirty, he stood and stretched out the kinks.

Jason helped him to put everything away.

"You weren't bored?" Michael asked.

"I liked it. It was peaceful."

Peaceful. Good word for it.

Outside, the sun had already started its winter slide toward the horizon with the temperature dropping fast.

The snow hushed their footsteps back to the house.

Michael opened the door to a swell of sound, children's playful voices.

"Sounds like the kids are awake."

Jason smiled at him, man to man, as though they shared a private joke. *The children slept, but we had manly time.*

Michael was happy on a number of counts. One, that he'd given the boy adult male companionship. And two, that Jason's mother had given him the gift of quiet time, of a shot of solitude that even Jason's presence couldn't dim.

In fact, Jason had had a calming effect on him, like the steady heartbeat of the animals around him.

Michael worked to harden his defenses. Yeah, Samantha had done something good for him. Still didn't mean he wanted her here.

After an early dinner, Michael and Samantha carried their dirty dishes into the kitchen.

"We've got three hours until bedtime." Michael looked frazzled. The kids had been barely manageable throughout dinner. "What now?"

"We're going to put on a show," Samantha announced.

He frowned. "A show? What do you mean?"

"When my boys are bored, sometimes I make them get creative and make up a story and act it out."

"Lily's too young. I don't think she can do that."

"I know." She spread her hands. "I don't know what else to do. We could watch TV, I guess."

"I don't know how much diesel I want to use on entertainment. The problem is we don't know how long this blackout will last. We've used a lot of fuel. Tomorrow, we might need our electricity to cook more food."

"I understand," Samantha said. "So let's try my idea. The worst that can happen is that the show won't be any good, but we'll pass some time and the kids will be entertained."

He nodded. "Let's do it."

She stepped into the living room and made her announcement.

Colt asked, "What kind of show?"

"How about a play?"

"About what?"

"I don't know. We have to write it."

"I can't write yet, Mom."

Samantha scrubbed Colt's hair. "I know that, honey. I'll write it down, but we all have to come up with ideas."

"Ideas for what?" Mick asked.

"For a story. No worries. I'll guide you every step of the way. The first thing we have to decide is what type of story we want. How about a romance?"

She'd said the last to elicit exactly the response she got. Jason groaned and the younger boys rolled their eyes.

"You don't like that idea?" she asked, stifling a laugh.

"How about cops and robbers?" Mick said.

"How about soldiers?" Colt asked.

Samantha shuddered at both suggestions. There would be guns involved. She hated guns.

"Fairy princesses," Lily said.

"Yuck. No way. Boys don't dress like princesses. That's a dumb idea."

"Colt, behave," Samantha warned. "No one's ideas are dumb just because they don't suit us."

Mick hovered protectively near his sister.

Nice to see, but Sammy wanted to foster a sense of self and independence in the little one while she was here.

"How about a compromise? What about a Western?" She had an idea of where she could go with it. "Everyone could dress up in things you probably already own."

"Yeah!" Mick and Colt shouted.

"But..." she said, stalling them with a raised hand. "There will be *no* guns."

"But—"

"Cowboys—"

She cut off their complaints. "We'll use cardboard swords. It will be a swashbuckling Western."

"Can we have masks like Zorro?" Mick asked, getting into the spirit.

"Can we have capes?" Colt asked.

"Yes to both."

The boys cheered.

Okay. So far, so good. They were off to a strong start. *Let's see how far their pent-up energy takes them*, Samantha thought.

Jason watched his mother quietly. He knew her well. He'd probably already guessed she had an idea where the story was going to go.

"Mick," she said, "We're not going to let your father know anything about the play until we put it on tonight, okay? We'll practice while he does his chores."

"Mom," Jason said, touching her arm. "Can I help Michael instead of being in the play?"

Samantha stroked his cheek. "You like working with the animals, don't you?"

"Yeah, Mom. I really like it. Please?"

Samantha glanced at Michael where he sat on the sofa with a ranching magazine open on his lap. He'd stopped reading and was watching her.

He nodded. "He's a good helper. He does a great job."

The man couldn't have done anything better to endear himself to her than to praise one of her sons.

"Okay." She smiled at Jason. "You're off the hook. You and Michael will be the audience. The rest of you, come with me."

Before Michael left the house, she said, "Give us half an hour more with the electricity. You can turn it off for the show and the rest of the night."

He nodded and headed out.

Michael's bedroom became Command Central. They pulled together anything that could be used to make costumes for the boys and dumped it onto the bed.

Using aluminum foil over cardboard, she helped the children to fashion swords.

She explained to them what the story was about.

"But, Mom," Colt protested. "That's not fair."

"Not another word, Colt. You get to be one of the bad guys. You'll have fun."

Charmed that Michael had thought to bring her suitcase from the car, Samantha pulled out a bathrobe and put it on over the bedsheet she was using as her costume. She would take it off in time for the play.

At the back door, she put two fingers to her lips and whistled.

"That's mom," Jason said.

"That was her?"

Jason nodded. Sounded pretty powerful to Michael.

"It means she's ready. Let's go."

On the walk back to the house under a cold, starlit sky, Michael asked, "Are these shows usually any good?"

"Yeah. Mom's really great at this."

Michael stepped in through the back door after Jason and secured it for the night.

Behind his closed bedroom door, he heard giggling.

Samantha called, “Can you turn off the generator and start the fire? We need the lanterns lit, too.”

“Sure.” He asked Jason to handle the fire, making the boy light up with pride.

“Which end of the room is supposed to be the stage?” he asked Samantha through his closed door.

“The end away from the fire.”

Michael positioned four lamps around the room to light up that end.

“Done,” he called out.

“You and Jason sit on the air mattresses in front of the fire so you have a good view.”

They did and waited.

First down the hallway were Mick and Colt, looking more like swashbuckling pirates than cowboys, with towels for capes, full of high spirits.

“We’re the bad guys,” Mick shouted.

“We’re bastardly villains,” Colt said.

From down the hallway came Samantha’s voice. “Dastardly!”

“That’s what I said, Mom.”

Samantha laughed, that gay tinkle that had captivated Michael her first day here.

The boys play-fought for a while until Samantha called, “Hey, yoo-hoo. The damsel in distress is waiting, bad guys.”

"Oh, yeah."

"We forgot."

They ran back down the hallway and returned, forcing Samantha ahead of them at sword-point.

Michael startled.

This was a different Samantha than he'd seen. He'd thought his first glimpse of her beauty had stolen his breath, but *this* Samantha...

Her classically sculpted face with huge blue eyes framed by a cloud of white-blond hair might be pure innocence, but her body was pure femme fatale.

A white bedsheet clung to every curve as though caressing her. One of his belts cinched a tiny waist, but her hips flared below.

Good God. Michael couldn't stop staring, fool that he was, taken in by a woman's beauty when the physical had never mattered to him before, not since he'd fallen in love with a funny, irreverent, sweet girl named Lillian.

To him, beauty had never been any more of an asset than brains or brawn or talent. People were given gifts at birth, and they used them or didn't.

What mattered in the end was what you did with your life, how you treated the people around you and whether you could be strong enough for the hand life dealt you.

His mother and sister had valued beauty more than familial love and loyalty.

But Samantha stood on stage now as though her beauty were no more special than her intelligence or her personality.

It just *was*.

Spellbound, speechless, Michael stared. Gulped. Stared some more.

Finally, he clued in to the gist of the play.

"Please, kind sirs, don't hurt me," Samantha wailed with the back of one hand against her forehead.

Jason leaned close and whispered, "Mom's a terrible actress."

Michael nodded, mute. She couldn't act worth a damn, but she sure was pretty to watch.

"Help," she called.

A high, thin banshee wail startled Michael. His tiny daughter came running with a sword in her hand and a fierce determination on her tiny face.

"I'll save you, damned distress!"

"Damsel in distress," Samantha muttered.

Michael laughed. How could he not?

His sweet, timid daughter launched herself at the boys with her toy sword and vanquished them, mostly because the boys let her after a stern look from Samantha.

"Thank you, oh fierce and wonderful Lily! You have saved me and conquered our enemies." She grabbed Mick's sword and touched it to each of Lily's shoulders. "I dub thee Knight Lily."

"Hey," Jason said. "There aren't any knights in Westerns." His voice rang with humor.

"There are in this one." She placed Lily in front of her. She held out her hands to the boys, who took them. "Thank you, ladies and gentlemen, for attending this evening's entertainment."

They took a bow together.

Jason jumped to his feet and applauded loudly.

When Michael didn't stand quickly enough, the boy nudged his ankle and leaned down. "Mom always expects a standing ovation."

Michael jumped to his feet. "Bravo," he shouted, and the actors took it as their due.

"Hot chocolate for everyone!" Samantha said. "Go get ready for bed while I make it."

She scooted down the hallway and returned minutes later. She'd covered her bedsheet dress with a thick bathrobe. He could have wept on the spot.

While she poured milk into a big pot and added hot chocolate mix, he watched her back.

She'd put her hair up into some kind of bun. Wisps of it had fallen down around her neck. He wanted to touch them. That was all. Just feel them. Were they as silky as they looked?

With the pot in her hand, she turned around and caught him staring.

Her cheeks turned a delicate pink.

He couldn't find his tongue, struck speechless by an almost adolescent shyness.

The silence lengthened.

She opened her mouth to say something, but he cut her off with a raised hand, afraid she would ruin the moment with chatter.

She didn't like silence.

He did.

To lighten the mood, he said, "Awful lot of swearing for a children's play."

She laughed and he was glad. She relaxed into her natural self instead of the nervous woman who had to fill every gaping hole.

"The children were funny, weren't they?"

"Yeah. You were right. This putting-on-a-show business was good for them."

She shrugged, as if taking praise were uncomfortable for her. "It passed the time."

"It did that, yes."

"Will you put this on the fire while I get dressed?" Before leaving the room, she said, "Thank you for bringing in my clothes."

He would miss her wearing his sweats, but her gratitude warmed him.

In the living room, he placed the pot on the rack over the fire and listened to his daughter chatter away in his bedroom with Samantha.

His little girl, who spent too much time being solemn and quiet, was happy. *Happy.*

He sat back on his heels with the stunning realization that he'd just fallen a tiny bit in love with a woman he barely knew.

In a daze during the last hour before bedtime, Michael contemplated what to do about it.

Nothing, Moreno. Not a damned thing.

He fed the fire for the last time that night and crawled under his blankets on the sofa.

Everyone settled and the room quieted. All slept, except for Michael, who lay on his back staring at flickering shadows on his ceiling.

An hour later, he fed the fire again, took his blankets and quilts from the sofa and trudged down the hallway to the spare bed in his son's room. He couldn't face his own bed knowing that Samantha had slept in it a few nights before.

He couldn't sleep in the same room as her

tonight. He knew that all he had was a powerful case of lust, but it felt like more. An unwelcome flame flickered back to life.

When he closed his eyes, all he saw was a temptress in a white gown and a body made for his hands.

Self-disciplined, he could deal with it, but he needed the physical distance and the chill in the room to cool his blood.

Yep. This was a bad case of trouble he didn't need.

Chapter 8

Samantha felt the loss when Michael left the room. She hadn't heard him go, but something had disturbed her and she immediately missed his presence.

She wished he would stay.

She was safe in this house, and so were the children, but nighttime wreaked its havoc on her here as much as it had every night for the past two years since the trouble had started with Manny.

She got up and strode to Michael's bedroom, the meager light from the fire flickering behind her. He wasn't there.

Peeking into Mick's room, she spotted

his bulk on the single bed opposite the bunk beds. At least he was still in the house.

She turned to go back to the living room, but his deep voice stopped her.

"What's wrong?" Even in the darkness, he'd sensed her here.

"Nothing." But she couldn't help but wring her hands. If only morning would come.

"There is something wrong," he said, "but it's not the kids."

She shook her head, even though he couldn't see. "It's not the children. It's me."

His bulk changed shape as he sat up. "Tell me."

She felt her way toward Mick's bed and sat on the lower bunk, hauling a sheet up and around her shoulders. It was cool back here. Why had he left the warm living room?

She sat on her hands. She'd never told anyone about her fears, not even Travis. So why consider opening up to a stranger?

Maybe because she'd been dying for someone to talk to. She'd been a burden to her brother when they were growing up. She wouldn't share any more of her burdens with him, not after he'd already done more than any brother should. He'd sacrificed his adolescent dreams and his own happiness to raise her.

"I don't like nighttime," she told the dark figure across from her.

"Why not?"

Michael's voice sounded as deep and strong as he looked in the daytime.

"I'm afraid."

"Why?"

"It started in high school. Our parents had died and Travis worked hard to take care of both of us so I wouldn't have to go to foster care."

He made a low humming sound in his throat. She didn't know what it meant.

"He's the best brother ever," she whispered fervently.

"Sounds like."

"He often worked late at night. At first he was still trying to go to school, so he would wash dishes in restaurants or bars. I didn't like being alone so much. I hated it."

"How old were you?"

"Only twelve. I know he was always there for me, but on those nights, I felt abandoned. When I was alone in the tiny apartment with only the lock on the door to protect me, every sound was terrifying."

"Makes perfect sense." She sensed him leaning forward. "Nothing, I mean, *nothing* can hurt you here. Understand?"

Although she knew he couldn't see her, she nodded. "I know."

And she did know. He wouldn't let anyone hurt a soul in this house.

She cupped one hand inside the other, squeezing hard, and debated whether to tell him the rest, about Manny and the trial. But what good would that do? He would only worry, and there was no threat.

Manny had said he would never bother her again. She believed him.

The only thing bothering her now was her imagination.

She wished she knew Michael well enough to take shelter in his arms, but she wouldn't.

The only thing she had ever done wrong with men was to give too soon.

She'd done it with Kevin, thinking that he was her chance to have a real family in a real house. She'd been wrong.

Just before all of the trouble with Manny, there had been Greg. She'd moved along too quickly with him, too, only to find he'd wanted her body, but nothing else.

She stood up. "Thank you for listening."

"Yeah," he said, and she left the room, wishing she could stay, but knowing she couldn't.

* * *

Michael awoke in a lousy mood. He knew the reason—Samantha and her midnight confession.

He didn't want her to have depth and to be thoughtful, vulnerable and...*likable*, for God's sake.

Why couldn't she be as shallow as his assumptions about beautiful women needed her to be?

He didn't want to soften or yield.

Silently, he and Jason did their chores, the boy a welcome distraction from his confused musings.

They hopped onto the snowmobile in the brightening dawn and checked out cattle, feed and water. Jason soaked it all up like a load of hay in the rain.

When they returned to the house, a rustling in the living room alerted him to the gradual stirring of his children and his guests.

Going immediately to the fireplace, he didn't look at Samantha until he'd finished his chore, then regretted peeking at her.

She looked sleep-mussed, her hair a cloud of blond tangles and her cheek creased from her pillow. The fact that she didn't cater to her looks was another strike against her in his books. It made her even more appealing and he didn't want that.

When she saw him, her face creased into a smile that had his defenses crumbling without a sound.

Shattered, he spun away.

No. He would *not* let this happen to his heart, in his house, under Lillian's roof.

Grumbling, he stalked to the kitchen to raid their dwindling supplies.

A small missile launched herself at his legs, his pretty daughter with her delicate face and big hair. He picked her up. Prone to grumpiness in the morning, today Lily smiled sweetly and said, "Love you, Daddy."

He almost regretted the development and refinement of her speech, missing the funny appeal of her former "Wuv you."

"Love you, too, sweetheart."

With her head on his shoulder, she giggled and placed her palm against his chest. "Rumbly."

"What are you so happy about, sprout?"

Her shoulders hunched up around her ears and she giggled again. "Just happy, Daddy."

He knew why. Samantha. The company. The fun and lightness and activity of the past two and a half days and three nights.

Had the past two years been too gloomy

for his children? Hadn't he done his best to provide for them?

It hadn't been enough. This woman had waltzed in and changed everything.

He didn't resent his children's happiness, but dear God, how many barriers was Samantha going to crash through?

He wasn't ready for this. He wasn't ready for *anything.*

Samantha regretted having been so frank with Michael last night.

He'd been strange all morning. Something about him had shifted for sure. He wasn't as cold, as rigid or as gloomy, and yet he seemed more distant. From her, at any rate.

Maybe she'd said too much last night. Once again, she'd moved too quickly with a man, even when she had no designs on him. She'd just wanted someone to talk to.

Poor guy.

She couldn't wallow. There were children to take care of and to entertain.

At least after the fun of yesterday's snowball fight and last night's play, Michael was more relaxed with the children.

After breakfast, he said, "Remember that plane on the table inside the front door, Colt?"

"The one without wings?"

"That's the one. Go get it."

Colt ran off.

"Mick and Jason, find me a couple of chunks of firewood that are relatively flat."

The other boys checked the wood piled beside the hearth.

When everything was assembled, Michael set it all up on the coffee table on top of a couple of towels.

Samantha settled on the sofa.

Michael said, "Boys, gather round the table. I'll show you how to use a plane."

Michael knelt in front of the coffee table and the boys clustered around him.

Lily came to sit beside Samantha.

Sammy brooded. Why hadn't Lily been invited to watch as well?

Lily curled against Sammy's side, combing Puff's hair as Sammy had shown her. First, Sammy had had to get all of the tangles out for her.

The child hummed a formless tune.

Michael started in on his lesson. Samantha frowned, thoughtful. Sure it was great that he was teaching the boys how to use it, but it would have been doubly nice if he'd thought to include his daughter.

There was no reason girls couldn't learn how to use tools if they wanted to.

Don't worry about it, Sam. You won't be here much longer. Another day at the most.

But she did worry, and she brooded.

Don't get involved. Michael gets upset if he thinks you're criticizing him as a parent.

It was none of her business, but the unfairness ate away at her.

Lily deserved so much. She deserved everything. She was sweet and—

Stop, Sammy! In the end, Lily is none of your business.

She bit her lips shut. She sat on her hands.

Who was she kidding? She could not sit here quietly and let Lily be left out. She gave up resisting.

Travis always said she had too much mischief in her heart. She tried to make life fun for her boys, to make up for all of the years when things had been anything but fun for her and Travis.

She had enough self-awareness to know she was projecting the slights she'd felt in her childhood onto Lily, but she also felt that Michael really should have included the girl.

Boys should be taught domestic skills and girls should be taught anything mechanical they could get their hands on.

She bent down and whispered into Lily's

ear, detailing precise instructions on what she was supposed to do.

Lily grinned, nodded and slipped down from the sofa like a miniature wraith, sneaking behind the males huddled around the coffee table with exaggerated footsteps.

Lily couldn't have been more obvious if she tried. Samantha struggled to hold in her laughter.

Fortunately, the males were so engrossed with their tools they didn't notice, not until the moment Lily jumped onto her father's back.

"Wha—?"

Lily giggled.

"Sammy said you should show me, too, not just the boys."

His deep brown gaze shot to Sammy. She raised one eyebrow, daring him to object.

With a wry twist of his lips, he acknowledged the rightness of it. "Touché."

To his daughter, he said, "Sorry, honey. Sammy's right. I should have included you. Come stand here beside me."

She wrapped her arms across the front of his throat and rested her cheek against his.

"I stay here, Daddy."

Across the coffee table, Samantha heard his breathing hitch.

"That's a good spot for you, Lily," Michael murmured while a soft smile tinged his lips. "The best."

Over the next twenty minutes, he exhibited an extreme level of patience. The children had a lot of questions and all wanted to try their hands at planing wood.

All except Lily. She seemed to value the physical closeness to her father more than the lesson.

When the lesson and the children's interest had run its course, Michael stood, carrying his daughter on his back, fists on his hips just below Lily's legs.

With his solid stance and muscled legs, his thighs filling his jeans, he looked indomitable.

Strong. Utterly trustworthy. Dependable.

Safe.

Michael had good thighs. Samantha liked thighs, loved to curl with a man after making love, with one of his thighs snuggled between hers.

With one hand, Michael scratched his head. "Has anyone seen Lily? I swear she was here a minute ago."

Her head ducked down behind his shoulder and she giggled against his back.

He spun around. "I can hear her, but I can't see her."

Lily burst into full-blown laughter and a light came into Michael's eyes that Sammy hadn't seen before.

He wrapped one strong arm around his back and hauled his daughter forward and across his chest. He blew loud, messy raspberries into the crook of her neck. Lily squealed.

Lifting her high and tossing her into the air, he laughed like an oversize, oh-so-manly boy.

Michael turned to Samantha and grinned.

Her heart stopped running blood into her veins. Her whole body seemed to pause.

Michael Moreno's smile made him downright beautiful. A dazzling light shone from him, at once deepening his dark eyes and lighting them with a powerful energy. White teeth flashed against tanned skin. His jaw and cheekbones seemed to soften and become accessible and touchable.

Her fingers itched. Oh, how they itched. Her skin tightened.

It had been too long. Kevin had checked out early in their marriage, his travels and his search for self more important than anything else.

Colt had been a last-ditch effort to save the

marriage. It hadn't worked, but she thanked her lucky stars he'd been born.

Her boys were her saving grace.

Her husband hadn't touched her after Colt's birth, had simply told her that carnal pursuits messed with his spiritual journey. His body was a holy temple.

Maybe, but so was hers, and her temple needed sexual gratification now and again.

More than that, her body needed physical affection. She craved a good cuddle as much as she wanted sex.

Greg had never understood that. He'd been a main-event kind of guy. She regretted becoming involved with him. Thank God it had only been one night before she realized how shallow he was. She deserved better. She knew that now.

Mick grasped his father's arm. "Me, too, Dad."

Sammy saw a longing in Mick that broke her heart. There was too much sadness in this house.

Michael's smile froze, as though he'd come to the same conclusion. He put down his daughter and picked up his son.

It took more effort to toss the larger child into the air and catch him, but Michael did.

His biceps strained against his long-sleeved

shirt. He'd rolled them to his elbows, and sinews popped beneath his skin, emphasizing his power.

Michael kissed his son loudly on the cheek and set him onto his feet.

When he picked up Colt, he compounded her distress, her attraction to him. Colt had been clinging to his pant legs. Michael played with him as easily as he had with his own kids.

Jason hovered nearby watching the antics, too big to toss into the air, but still young enough to want to have fun.

As well, Sammy knew how much he missed his father's presence in his life. More than Colt did. For Colt, his father's disappearing act had been part of his life, but Jason could remember a time when his dad had made an effort to be a father. A small one, but enough to leave Jason always wanting more.

While Samantha craved physical affection, a soft touch, a gentle caress, a hug now and then, so did Jason crave a father's hand on his shoulder. A father's hug.

Michael set Colt down, steadying him with a broad hand on the back of his head. He glanced at Jason, seemingly gauging his height.

"Sorry, kid," he said, "but you'd hit the ceiling if I tossed you. You're too big."

Jason put on a game face and shrugged, but Sammy knew what it cost him.

"But," Michael said, raising one finger, "you're not too big for this!"

Michael tossed Jason into an armchair and tickled him until the boy begged for him to stop. Halfheartedly. Jason came up grinning and happy.

Samantha hadn't seen that in a long, long time. Her eyes watered. It set her soul on fire. Her boys deserved more. They deserved a loving, *present* father and a safe home and security from a crook like Manny d'Onofrio.

His crimes, and the subsequent trial, had set her life behind. She had a plan, to make a real home for herself and her boys. To put down roots and surround them with love and stability for the rest of their childhoods.

She would take Travis's help for a little while longer and then she would blaze her own independent trail.

Today's respite from those two years of worry was good, except for the hero worship she saw on her son's face when he looked at Michael.

Michael might be severe and opinionated, but he showed sensitivity, too. Why couldn't he be a bad guy through and through and save her from this terrible ache?

She didn't want to admire him or want him.

Worse, she didn't want her son worshipping him or seeing him as a stand-in father. They would be here for another couple of days at the most and then they would leave to live with Travis…and his new family.

She knew her son well. Jason would miss Michael, even though he'd known him for only three days. How much deeper would their bond become over the next few days until they could leave? How much more difficult would it be for Jason when they did?

His life had been either about leaving people or about being left behind. This could only hurt him.

He would grieve yet again.

Michael smiled down at the children and Samantha's pulse beat harder.

Be careful, Samantha. Be so, so careful.

She could see herself falling into a trap with this man. That trap looked suspiciously like the answer to her prayers for a solid, dependable husband, a good home for her boys and a lifelong love that couldn't be shattered by egos.

The trap was her own desires, and her yearning for security.

Would she trade her happiness for her children's security? She already had. She'd stayed with her husband too long. But would she take on another man for that same security? No. She would provide for her children on her own. She would keep them safe.

Her loneliness could go take a hike. She would survive.

When she loved again, it would be for love itself and not for all of the accoutrements that *might* come with it.

If Sammy ever married again, it would be for good.

She wouldn't put her children through another divorce. She wouldn't let them be hurt again.

She would never, ever let herself *fall* into another relationship.

Clapping his hands, Michael said, "Who's hungry?"

The children screamed, "Me!"

"Me, too!"

"Me, three!"

Michael led them to the kitchen while Samantha stayed behind and, one by one, killed every good feeling and thought she had toward Michael Moreno.

After lunch they got the kids outside again. They had another snowball fight at the front of the house, but no one was ready to go back inside. Not quite yet.

Samantha stared into the brilliance of another flawless sunny day. Mick and Cody ran down the shoveled path. Jason followed, giving Lily a piggyback ride.

Soon, she thought, *this crazy, stressful, amazing idyll will come to an end, but not today.*

She saw Michael lean into his snow fort trough and crouch there. *He's making more snowballs.*

No *way* was she letting him get the upper hand on her and her team.

She sneaked up behind him with a handful of snow to shove down his neck, but somehow he heard her and spun around.

She laughed and tried to smash the snow onto his face, but he grasped her wrist.

Together, they rolled in the snow.

They wrestled until they were breathless. Samantha kept in shape and was strong, but Michael was a force of nature.

It didn't help that she couldn't stop laughing.

Michael ended up on top of her, blocking out the endless sky and holding her wrists.

Her laughter stilled. So did his. He stared, eyes dark and unreadable. A small frown furrowed his brow, as though he, too, didn't know what this was about.

His heavy body pressed down on hers. His solidity felt like heaven.

A blob of snow dropped from his hat onto her cheek. He leaned in slowly, giving her time to object. She held her breath and closed her eyes, the precious discipline she'd fought so hard for earlier gone on a puff of wind as though it had never existed.

Sammy, you are in so much trouble.

A moment later, his warm mouth kissed the snow from her cheek.

She recognized it for what it was. A halting uncertain beginning, an exploration and a question.

Is this okay?

Yes.

Enchanted, she opened her eyes and found his chocolate gaze studying her, confusion clear in his face. She understood. She felt the same way.

She hadn't come here looking for love or romance. She had come to ensure the safety of her boys. Instead, she'd discovered this sad man tucked away with his sad children.

As aloof as he'd been this morning, she expected more of the same treatment, but some of his reserve had broken when he'd played with the children.

When he started to move away from her, Samantha stopped him.

"Wait!" He still held her wrists. "Let go."

He did. With one hand she held on to the lapel of his jacket. She needed to explore this. Maybe there was something here. This man wasn't her ex. Michael seemed honest and reliable, and her body couldn't deny his physical appeal.

With her other hand, she dipped her mitten into the snow and swiped it across her cheek, leaving it cold and wet.

"Again," she whispered.

A slow, sweet-but-knowing smile tipped up the corners of his mouth.

He leaned close again, his breath warm on her skin. He licked her cheek, his tongue warm against the frosty chill of the air. She closed her eyes and sighed. It had been so long since a man had touched her with tenderness.

She knew plenty about men and lust, but tenderness? Not so much.

Ever since she'd developed this body that was both a blessing and a curse, she'd grown used to men wanting her, but she liked a side of affection with her sex. If not love, then at the very least warmth.

She'd been starving.

Tenderness emanated from Michael in waves. He not only desired her. He also liked her. That made all the difference in the world.

His lips trailed down her cheek to her mouth. She parted her lips to invite him in.

The shouts of the children brought her back to reality.

"Oh!" She'd forgotten about them. She *never* forgot about her sons. With a surge of panic, she pushed hard against Michael's chest. He fell over into the snow. It billowed up around him, coating him.

He looked so bewildered, one minute holding a warm and willing woman and the next flat on his back in the snow. A laugh huffed out of Samantha.

The kids laughed, too, breaking the moment. Michael helped her out of the snow and they all went inside for lunch, but Sammy's lips still tingled with anticipation of a kiss, and her cheek held the memory of his exploration. Her breath still felt the mingling of his, the intertwining of the softest of intimacies.

Michael Moreno packed a powerful punch when he allowed his soft, tender side to show. What on earth would he be like in bed?

* * *

After lunch, two things happened at once.

The first thing they all heard at the same time. A rumbling from down the road.

"What is it?" Samantha asked.

Michael had been strange since that almost-kiss, one minute staring at her with wonder and the next surly.

At the moment, he looked unhappy. "It's the plow."

She ran to the window. "Children, look!"

A plow made its way down the road, sending huge plumes of snow into the air to pile high onto the edges of fields.

"Pretty," Lily squealed.

It was quite a spectacle. The kids rejoiced.

Then the phone rang.

"I guess we have power," Michael said. He answered the phone. "Yes, Karen, we're fine. No, we don't need you to come out. Really, no, don't come. We've been good."

After some more mumbling, he hung up and flicked on a lamp.

Staring at Samantha, he said, "It's over."

She understood. *Everything* was over. Not just the aftermath of the snowstorm and the power outage, but also whatever that almost-something was that had happened outside in the snow.

Saved by the plow.

Reality had returned and Samantha welcomed it. Truly she did.

Honest.

Whatever had nearly started between them had been nothing more than the product of too-intense forced intimacy. This house had been a crucible and they'd crept too close to the flame.

They'd been thrown into an unusual situation and they'd been tempted, that was all.

Real life beckoned. Whatever they'd had here could never survive in the real world. They were too different. Opposites, really.

"Guess I'd better call the garage about towing your car," Michael mumbled.

She nodded, unsure what to say. She'd never experienced anything like this before in her life.

A little under four days ago, they'd been strangers. Imagine that.

"I guess I should call Travis about coming to get us."

Michael nodded.

Lily stood between them, looking first at one and then the other of them, picking up on the tremors of change.

Her lower lip trembled. "Daddy?"

Michael picked her up. "It's time for Samantha and the boys to go to their own home."

"No," she said, voice small, but forceful. "Don't want them to go."

"We have to let them go. They don't belong here. They belong with Travis."

They don't belong here.

He'd made that clear from the start, hadn't he? But for a few precious hours, things had felt different.

"No. Not yet, Daddy. Amorrow."

"I'm afraid not, sweetheart."

Samantha glanced at the boys. Mick and Colt looked bewildered and sad. Jason looked crushed.

She made a snap decision. Meddling one last time in this family's life, she was doing it for her boys, too. And for herself.

"I have an idea."

"You always do." Again, Michael was back to the grim smiles, but maybe his eyes shone a bit. "What is it?"

"How about one last supper together? One more night. This is a shock. Let's say good-bye gradually, tomorrow morning."

Michael nodded slowly. "We could do that."

"We need groceries. We've been scraping the bottom of the barrel on fresh items. We need milk, apples, cheese."

"Write up a list and I'll drive into town."

He should have been happy. He hadn't wanted them here, but he looked as torn as she felt.

This should be reason to celebrate. Then let's celebrate, she thought.

"We have three apples left. I'll make us a cake and we'll celebrate meeting each other and having this amazing adventure together, okay?"

The boys nodded. Lily hid her face against her father's shoulder.

The appeal in Jason's eyes when he asked Michael if he could go into town with him tore at Samantha.

Michael nodded. Mick and Colt wanted to go, too. Michael nodded again.

"Make the list," he said. "What about you?" he asked Lily. "You coming?"

She shook her head. "Want to stay with Sammy."

Samantha reached for her and Lily fell limply into her arms.

Using a riding snowblower, Michael cleared the driveway then backed his pickup truck out of the garage.

The subdued group left ten minutes later

after collecting Colt's booster seat from Samantha's car and transferring it to Michael's pickup truck.

Chapter 9

Bereft without the boys and Michael, Samantha put on her happy hat, as she'd had to do so many times in the past when Kevin had left her and the boys behind.

"Let's bake a cake! Would you like that?"

Lily nodded. "With apples, Sammy?"

"Yes, and cinnamon."

"I like cimmamim."

Over the next half hour, they put together a fragrant cake batter. Sammy could have done it in half the time on her own, but it was too much fun working with Lily to set her aside and take over completely.

They had a snack and cleaned up, Lily poking in her little head wherever it was in the way the most. Sammy loved it.

Oh, she was going to miss her.

Don't think about that.

"What would you like to do now?"

Lily looked tired, but their time together was nearly at an end, so Samantha didn't even bother to suggest a nap.

"Want to read picture books," Lily said.

"Okay. Where are they?"

"In my bedroom."

In her room, Lily pointed to a couple of large photo albums on a shelf. Sammy took them down.

"You mean real pictures."

"Mommy's picture books." Swinging Puff up from the bed by her hair, the girl slapped her doll against her chest and held on tightly. The more tired Lily was, the more attached she became to her doll.

Walking back to the living room, Sammy wondered what she would find in the albums.

They sat close together on the sofa and Samantha opened the top book. There in the first plastic sleeve was a glossy eight-by-ten of Michael on his wedding day, wearing a black suit, white shirt and black tie with a silver buckle inset with turquoise stones.

She might not be familiar with Western

culture and rural Montana, but she'd seen enough cowboys in the hotels in Vegas to recognize what they wore. The tie was a bolo. She liked the design of it.

Black cowboy boots completed the look.

Samantha recognized the front of Michael's ranch house. Long rays of morning sunlight shone full blast on him. A breeze threw a lock of thick brown hair over his forehead, creating a grown-up version of Mick.

A wide smile lit his face.

It was a wedding photo, but it looked more like a snapshot.

His smile, a luminous smile she'd never seen before, was directed at the photographer.

What Samantha saw in his gaze took her breath away.

Michael might not be happy now, might in fact be the grumpiest man she'd met in ages, and he might not know how to express his feelings, but he knew how to love.

That much was obvious in the way he looked at the photographer behind the camera.

His dark eyes glowed with love and pride.

"Daddy," Lily whispered.

"Yes." She guessed him to be about twenty or so.

"He's handsome," Sammy murmured.

She turned the page. A young woman stood in the same spot Michael had in the previous photo. In her eyes was a love that matched Michael's. So, he was the photographer this time.

Samantha smiled. The woman wasn't quite centered in the shot and the top of her hair was almost cut off. Michael wasn't as skilled behind the camera as his wife.

Yes, Samantha had no doubt this was Michael's wife. Her long, simple dress of ivory lace flowed over a petite figure to touch her off-white patent leather shoes.

A circlet of small purplish-pink flowers sat on her honey hair, which fell long and natural over her shoulders.

She looked even younger than Michael.

"Mommy," Lily said.

"What was her name?"

Lily stared at Samantha for a moment and then frowned. "Mommy," she repeated.

Lily probably had no idea what her mother's given name was.

"She's in heaven. She's a angel now."

Sammy wrapped her arm around Lily. "A beautiful angel."

Lily nodded.

Although an ordinary woman with plain features, her face glowed. The love that streamed from her toward Michael made her beautiful.

The next photo was of the two of them together on the steps of a small church, surrounded by people she guessed were friends and family. Cowboy hats and bolo ties abounded.

These were more formal shots taken by a professional, but the nicest by far were the sweet early-morning photos they had taken of each other.

"Wanna see something pretty?" Lily asked.

"Yes. Is it another photograph?"

"No. Come."

Samantha followed the child to her bedroom, where Lily opened the small drawer of her bedside table and pulled out a Christmas tree ornament, of all things.

A tiny Santa Claus held a baby. On the baby's blanket was inscribed the name *Lily* and *Love from Mama*.

"Oh, Lily," Samantha breathed. "It's beautiful."

Lily nodded. "Pretty."

"Does this go on your Christmas tree every year to remind you of your mother?"

Lily shook her head.

"You keep it in your room? You don't hang it on your tree?"

"Don't have a tree."

"What do you mean? You don't have a *Christmas* tree?"

Lily shook her head again.

"It isn't one of your traditions?"

"What does *tradshun* mean?"

"It means…" Samantha struggled to explain. "It's what you do every year at Christmastime. The same things every year. If you don't have a tree, what do you do for Christmas?"

Lily looked at her solemnly. "We don't do nothing, Sammy."

Stunned by Lily's statement, Samantha couldn't even correct the child's grammar. *"Nothing?"*

"No. Daddy says it doesn't matter. All days are the same."

Samantha staggered out through the doorway, down the hall and to the living room where she grabbed one of the photo albums. Flipping through the pages, she didn't stop until she found what she was looking for. Photographs of Christmas.

There. In one of them was a tree, covered in ornaments. Samantha peered closely and spotted Lily's little Santa with the baby.

In another photo, Lily's mother stood in front of the tree holding a tiny baby in a pink blanket. In another, she looked younger and held a baby wrapped in a blue blanket. Mick.

So Christmas *used* to be celebrated in this house.

Lily had joined her and stood quietly watching.

"Lily?" Samantha asked.

"Yes, Sammy?"

"Do you remember if you had Christmas last year?"

"I don't memember, Sammy. I was just little."

"Yes, true. You would have been so tiny then." Samantha patted Lily's head. "Not like the big girl you are now."

Idly, thinking, she ran her fingers through Lily's thick dark hair. "Would you like to have Christmas?"

Lily nodded so hard her barrette went flying.

Samantha picked it up and secured a lock off Lily's forehead. "Would you like to have a Christmas tree?"

"Yes!" she yelled almost as loudly as her brother would have.

Michael wouldn't like it. He'd already been angry with the meddling she'd done since she got here. But cripes. This was Christmas. This was important.

What had been happening in this house, with Michael either canceling or ignoring Christmas, had been a tragedy. An absolute tragedy.

Why on earth could the man not make the effort to have Christmas for his children?

Grief. Paralyzing grief.

She turned to the photograph of Michael on his wedding day. Kevin had never, not once in their marriage, looked at her with that depth of feeling.

Having known love that special, how must it feel to lose it?

Devastating. Poor Michael. She felt for him.

But Christmas! Children deserved to have Christmas.

Images flared, ebbed and flowed, memories of childhood and the absence of celebration in her home. Samantha was smart enough to know she was thinking about more than just Mick and Lily. She was thinking about herself and Travis, and all that they'd missed out on.

In her childhood, the problem had been parental indifference. Her parents just hadn't cared enough to make the effort.

Michael was different. He loved Lily and

Mick. Was he doing a lot for them? Yes. Was it enough? Maybe not.

She shouldn't butt in, but she would anyway.

The kids deserved the Christmas they'd missed.

Decision made, Sammy nodded. This family was getting a Christmas. She wouldn't tell Lily yet, though. Michael was going to fight her tooth and nail on this.

Samantha relished the challenge.

Michael had a boy hanging from each arm while Jason walked ahead.

They'd already filled the bed of the truck with groceries and were heading to the diner for lunch.

They all put on a good show of being happy, but who was Michael kidding?

He hadn't wanted them in his house. Now he didn't want them to go. Keeping them was unrealistic.

What was wrong with him?

That near-kiss with Samantha today had been a moment of lust. Not true. Honesty, as always, compelled him to dig deeper. It was more than lust. He liked her. He cared for her already, but how was that possible? It had merely been a second of loneliness gone out of control.

She'd lain soft beneath him in so many layers of clothing he could barely determine her contours. But he imagined sinking into her softness and forgetting pain, grief and responsibility. He'd imagined just *being*. Just being with a woman. Just being with Sammy.

That wasn't going to happen.

This town, these people…this was his real life, not a woman from Vegas, of all places.

Samantha was more than *a woman from Vegas*. As uncomfortable as her confession to him had been last night, he also admired that she'd reached out.

He just wished he didn't feel so confused. She and her boys had invaded his house. They would be gone tomorrow. Again, he would have the peace, quiet and order that he craved.

Oh, joy, Moreno. There's been enough order and quiet to last a lifetime. She brought you fun.

Shut up. I need peace.

The house is going to reek of peace. Enjoy your quiet house without these great kids and that amazing woman.

Sometimes he hated his conscience.

Jason kept his head high, but Michael knew the kid was hurting. He hoped like hell that

Travis had animals. The boy deserved to be around them. He was a natural.

What a great kid.

Maybe too great. Kids weren't meant to be perfect. When did Jason cut loose? Did he ever get into trouble? Did he ever put a foot wrong?

Kids should have the right to make mistakes and get into mischief.

Michael's parents had been tolerant, but also strict, so he knew there could be a balance. There had been in the early years at least, before his mom and sister had left.

Michael adored his daughter, but he still managed to raise her with reasonable restrictions and expectations.

Couldn't the same be done with Jason?

The kid didn't have to be perfect.

Lost in his thoughts, he didn't notice at first when Jason burst ahead of them down the sidewalk, running full-tilt.

Colt chased after him.

What the—?

Jason, tall for his age and gangly, threw himself into a man's arms and wrapped his legs around his waist.

The man, tall and broad-shouldered beneath his shearling coat, staggered a bit under Jason's weight, but managed to stay upright. The guy even laughed and hugged the boy hard.

Travis Read. Their uncle. Had to be.

Travis put Jason down and lifted Colt high, making the kid giggle. He tossed him and caught him.

Michael watched as Mick patted the man's leg. Not one to approach strangers easily, he probably thought if the man was okay with Jason and Colt, he would treat him well, too.

Travis looked down, put Colt on the ground and picked up Mick by his biceps, holding him at arm's length and smiling.

"Who do we have here?" he said with a slight smile.

"I'm Mick!" he shouted.

"He's our new friend," Colt said. "It sounds like he forgot to put in his hearing aids again."

Travis peeked in both of his ears. "Nope. No hearing aids. Any friend of Colt's is a friend of mine."

"Throw me, too!"

Travis looked past Mick to Michael with raised eyebrows that asked permission.

Michael nodded.

The man threw Mick into the air and caught him easily on the way down.

His son's giggles warmed Michael's heart.

Jason and Colt crowded Travis for his attention.

Michael took Mick from Travis and set him on his feet, saying, "Give the boys time with their uncle."

Mick watched the byplay between the boys and the man with a fascinated intensity. "What's an uncle?"

While the boys chatted with Travis, with Jason more animated than he'd been in Michael's house, Michael explained to Mick what an uncle was.

Since Michael's sister had left many years before Mick and Lily had been born, they didn't have an aunt. Maybe they had cousins, but Michael didn't know.

That was a whole story his kids would never hear, not if he had any say in the matter.

When the boys had settled, Travis reached out a hand. "You must be Michael Moreno. I'm Travis Read."

They shook. Travis had a good, hard handshake, hitting the right balance of managing confidence without aggression.

He reached out that same hand to Michael's son. "I'm Travis. Pleased to meet you."

Mick straightened and took the proffered hand.

Michael liked the man immediately for treating a boy as an equal.

"I'm real sorry my sister and the boys intruded on you."

It had been an intrusion. The woman had shaken up his world, had shattered his peace. He'd resented it. He'd resented *her*, but he couldn't tell Travis that.

Hell, to be fair, Samantha had done so much for them. "No problem. I had plenty of food. The boys are good kids. Quiet."

Travis grinned. "Not like Samantha. My sister's got a set of lungs that don't quit."

Michael grinned reluctantly.

Travis stared down at his nephews. The wistfulness on his face tugged at Michael and he realized this was the first the man had seen them in what? Months?

"We're taking advantage of the plowed roads to get more supplies."

Travis nodded. "Me, too."

Michael glanced around. The town wasn't too crowded yet. There was an empty table in the window of the diner.

He pointed to it. "You want to stop with us for a snack?"

"Yeah." Travis led the way inside and hung up his cowboy hat on the hooks that lined the wall beside the door.

"My favorite thing about this town when I

first arrived," he said, "was these hat hooks in every establishment."

Michael hung up his hat beside Travis's. Only a few of the hooks were in use. Other times, on busy days, you'd be hard-pressed to find an empty one.

"It's a great system," Michael said. "Hats don't get lost. They don't get crushed. They don't fall on the floor and get trodden on."

"Most surprising thing is that nobody steals anyone else's."

"Nope. That's a crime that isn't tolerated around here."

They managed to snag the window table, Jason and Colt on one side with Travis, and Mick on the other with Michael.

Violet Summer, the owner of the Summertime Diner, approached in her waitress's apron.

"Hey, where'd all these kids come from? I know Mick, but who are those big strapping boys beside you, Travis?"

"My nephews. This here's Jason, and that troublemaker in the corner is Colt."

Colt shrugged with a grin that matched his uncle's.

Michael smiled, because Samantha had said almost the same thing when they'd first arrived.

Colt seemed to like the attention.

"So," Vy said, setting one fist on a nicely rounded hip. She had a fine figure. Michael liked a woman with meat on her bones. "You finally arrived."

To Travis, she said, "Where's your sister? I'd love to meet her."

"They drove in through the snowstorm and got stuck. Fortunately, they were close enough to Michael's ranch to stop there."

Travis sobered. "Some of those roads are isolated. I'm glad your place was nearby. I don't know what would have happened to them if they'd been trapped in the car."

He didn't say out loud in front of the children what both he and Michael thought. The road-clearing crews could have made the sad discovery of a frozen woman and her two little ones.

Vy turned her attention to Michael. "They stayed at your place?"

He nodded. Inwardly, he smiled. Vy was the curious sort. She wasn't malicious, but he wasn't going to give her fuel for gossip.

"When did they get there?" she asked.

"Afternoon of the storm."

"Really?"

He nodded again.

"Travis's sister has been staying at your house for nearly four days?"

He nodded, biting the inside of his cheek so he wouldn't smile. Vy sure did like to dig for information.

"Like pulling teeth," she mumbled, disgruntled. She pointed to Travis and asked Michael, "Is she as pretty as this cowboy?"

Michael nearly laughed as Travis's cheeks turned bright red. What man wanted to be called *pretty*? What cowboy would tolerate it?

The longer Vy watched Michael, though, the more his own discomfort grew. Travis was a good-looking guy, but his sister had him beat in that department by miles.

As Michael had noticed multiple times every day since Samantha's arrival, she had a beauty unrivaled outside of pageants and Hollywood.

"Uh-huh, Vy," Mick piped up. "She's the prettiest woman on earth."

Maybe she was, Michael agreed. Probably.

He felt his own cheeks redden.

"Ohhhh," Vy said, infusing the simple word with all kinds of innuendo while his blush deepened. "*That* pretty, huh?"

Michael scowled. "Enough, Vy. Cut it out."

Ten years younger than him, she would

have been too young to remember what happened with his mother and sister.

His mother, with a fading beauty of her own, had been living out her onetime dream of stardom through her beautiful daughter.

Vy would never understand his aversion to beauty. She would only think his problem was that he was too attracted to Samantha.

Well, that was true, too, wasn't it?

Vy only laughed at his surliness. His bad humor slid from her like water off a chestnut's hide.

Relief came from an unexpected corner. His son. "She showed us how to make up plays."

"Plays?" Vy softened her attitude and said, "Imagine. She did a good job teaching you, did she?"

Vy could be a PITA in many ways, but she was truly kind to children. When Mick smiled proudly, Michael could have kissed the woman.

Putting on her waitress hat, Vy took their orders of pie, coffee and glasses of milk and left.

Michael listened to Jason and Colt bringing Travis up to date on all of their adventures since arriving at his ranch. He stared out the window.

Main Street slowly began to fill with people happy to be out after the enforced isolation of the storm.

As always, the town filled him with pride, or happiness, or a fair blend of both.

He knew every shop owner in town. Across the road, Jorgenson's Hardware and Hiram's Pharmacy and the only hairdressing salon in town, Nelly's 'Dos 'n' Don'ts, came to life.

Pickup trucks lined the curbs. This was a ranching community, and vehicles needed to do more than provide just transportation.

Townspeople sported plenty of leather cowboy boots and shearling coats and fur-based felt cowboy hats. *Put that in your pipe and inhale, city girl Samantha Read.*

He knew his surliness was a ploy to create the distance he was going to need to say goodbye to a pair of great kids and a woman he was starting to admire.

There was something to be said for self-defense.

This was ranching country. Samantha had come to the wrong place if she wanted to judge anyone who ate meat and wore animal products.

Let it go, he scolded himself. There would be time enough for grief and self-defense in the morning.

He realized Travis was staring at him.

"What?"

"I just asked what was happening with Samantha's car. Can she drive it to my house?"

Michael shook his head. "I called Artie Hanson about towing it to the garage, but he's got his hands full. Likely won't get out my way until tomorrow."

Travis's shoulders slumped. "I thought maybe she could come today. I've been waiting a long time for her and the boys to move in."

He brightened. "What am I thinking? I can come get them. The roads to my place are cleared. You just made it into town. No reason why I can't come out and get Sammy when we finish up here."

Mick asked, "Get Sammy?" He edged closer to his dad.

"Yeah, Mick. We knew they'd be leaving."

"But what about our celebration?"

"We'll have to have her and the boys out to the house another time. Okay? Travis wants them to come home with him now."

Why are you feeling so blue, Moreno? You wanted her gone from the moment she first set foot in your house.

"I don't want her to go," Mick said much too loudly. "She's fun."

"Samantha has to go," Michael said. "She came here to live with Travis."

"Jason and Colt, too?" Mick asked, peeved and not bothering to modulate his tone.

"Yep. Them, too."

Mick's expression turned mulish. A good kid, he had his stubborn side.

Travis watched the children with sympathy. "Y'all can come visit anytime you want."

"Yeah," Colt said. "Mick is my best friend. He has to come visit."

"Colt is my best friend, too," Mick said.

"It's a done deal," Travis said. "Give them a few days to settle in and then come visit."

Food arrived and everyone ate, but the mood had shifted. Samantha's kids seemed to have mixed feelings, happy to see their uncle at last, but already missing their new playmates before they'd even officially left them.

Michael's son was already missing the activity and vitality Jason and Colt had brought. He corrected himself almost immediately. The vitality was all Samantha.

Jason asked Travis, "How's your horse, Dusty?"

"Good. I checked him on the way into town. He's as restless as all the humans who've been snowbound by the storm. I need to get him out."

"I can help you feed him and brush him. You should see Michael's stable and his beautiful horses. Is your stable as big as his?"

"I don't have a stable yet. I have to build one in the spring."

Jason furrowed his young brow. "So where's Dusty?"

"Stabled at the Double U where I work."

"Oh." Jason deflated. "I thought he was at your house."

"We can stop in on him on the way home, if you like."

"'Kay." Jason started talking then about Michael's horses, naming each one and listing each unique characteristic. He rambled on about the work he'd been helping Michael with every morning, ending with, "We polished a bunch of tack, too."

Travis said, "Hey, that's great," but he looked vaguely annoyed.

When the man glanced at Michael, it struck him what the real problem was. Travis was jealous of the time Michael had had with the boy.

Nature and fate had conspired to put Travis's relatives in Michael's home when he didn't want them, and had deprived Travis of their first experiences in their new town.

There wasn't a damn thing either man could do about it.

After all of the pie was consumed, they paid and stepped outside the diner.

"How about if Jason and Colt ride with me and we'll come out to your ranch to get Samantha?"

"Now?"

What was the rush?

"Well, yeah," Travis responded. "Might as well. I'm here with the truck. I can fit them all in and put their luggage in the bed."

"Sure." Michael shrugged. "Could be done."

"Where are you parked?"

Michael gestured toward the black pickup at the far end of the street.

"I'm at the other end. Let me pull up behind you and follow you out."

"Colt's booster seat is in my truck."

"It's okay. I've got one in mine for Rachel's daughter."

Michael took Mick's hand and headed for his truck, while Travis took his nephews in the other direction.

To his shame, Michael drove home with a lead foot, on some level hoping he'd lose Travis, he guessed.

He shook his fool head.

What's that about, Moreno?

He slowed down.

At the ranch, he pulled up in the driveway and left Travis plenty of room to park behind him.

Travis and the boys followed him into the house.

It was quiet, too quiet, the way it used to be before these people barged in. It had become full of noise and energy and life.

The house smelled like cinnamon and apples and hominess. Their days of enforced isolation had felt long at times, but now seemed like they had barely started, as though they had been a dream. He knew he would miss them.

Jason called, "Mom, we're home and we have a surprise for you."

"What?" she called back, but to Michael's ear, something was wrong. He wasn't the most sensitive man around, but he knew when a woman sounded…off.

"What is it?" she said from the kitchen.

Samantha had a great voice, mellow and sexy, but she didn't sound like herself just now.

"Come here," Jason said. "You have to see."

She stepped into the hallway, looking a little sad. Worried about leaving? As he was worried about her having to leave, even though he shouldn't?

Then Samantha saw her brother and her face lit up like a hundred-watt bulb. The contrast hit Michael hard, even if she really meant nothing to him.

"Travis," she squealed, and threw herself into his arms. "I missed you. Oh my God, I missed you."

He spun her around. "Hey, sis. Good to see you."

Her voice, muffled against his shoulder, didn't sound right. Michael thought maybe she was crying.

His throat hurt, filled with an unaccustomed envy. He'd thought he used to have that kind of warm relationship with his little sister, but then she'd left without a backward glance. Was she even alive?

He should be happy for Travis and Samantha, because they seemed like decent people, but this was hard to watch.

He started to sidle into the living room, but Samantha turned to him. "Wait, please."

Glancing back, he asked, "Me?"

"Yes. We need to talk."

Talk? About what? He'd thought they were getting along. "What did I do?"

"Christmas," she whispered.

Christmas? He stiffened. He didn't do Christmas. Ever. Never again. Lillian had died just before Christmas. No. No Christmas. "What are you talking about?"

"You can't guess?" She looked sad and reproachful.

"I'm not a mind-reader."

"Hey, Sammy," Travis said. "I don't know what's going on, but if there's a problem with you staying here any longer, no worries."

Samantha turned her baby blues on her brother.

"What do you mean?" she asked Travis.

"I came to take you and the boys home."

"Home?" She seemed disoriented.

"Yeah. To the house I bought for you. For us."

"Oh. That home." She didn't sound too excited about it.

Travis hesitated. "Are you okay, Sammy?"

"Um..." She twisted her fingers. "I know you've waited a long time to show me the house, but I can't come right now."

"You can't come?" Travis sounded like a kid who'd lost his favorite toy. "But... But why not?"

Samantha pointed toward Michael and his two kids, who were both clinging to her legs. "Because of them."

No. No. Whatever she had in mind, just no. Whatever she was about to do would hurt him. He felt it in his bones.

"Wait a minute." Michael was overreacting. He didn't know what she was planning, but damn. She'd said *Christmas*. He couldn't catch his breath. He pushed against whatever was going on in her head.

Forcefully, he said, "I didn't do a darn thing to you other than take you in when you needed help. Don't interfere in my life."

"Don't yell at my sister," Travis shouted.

Lily burst into tears.

Samantha picked her up and rubbed her back. "Shh. Shh."

She raised a hand palm-out to the men and apologized. "I'm handling this badly."

"What is it, Sammy?" Travis asked quietly.

"I can't leave yet because…"

Michael watched Samantha as she seemed to gather her resources, or courage, or something.

"I need to stay a little longer, another week, because…" Again she hesitated and then blurted, "This family needs me."

Chapter 10

Stunned, Michael could only stare. What was she talking about? They didn't *need* her. *He* didn't need her.

Doubts niggled at him, though. Hadn't he stepped into this house not ten minutes ago and thought it was too quiet?

Hadn't he dragged his heels walking in knowing that soon those two great kids and their mother would be walking out?

No. He couldn't do this, couldn't need them. Couldn't need *her*.

He turned his back on Samantha and stormed into the living room.

He heard her say quietly, "Travis, I'm so sorry. Please trust me on this?"

Travis mumbled something, but Michael didn't catch it.

No wonder. He could barely hear a thing over the roaring in his ears.

Who did Samantha think she was to force herself onto him and his children for another week? He hadn't invited her. She hadn't asked. She'd made the decision on her own, meddling yet again.

Both of his children suddenly cheered. Okay, so maybe she wasn't forcing herself on them. They were happy she was staying.

But didn't he get a say in this?

Then her children cheered. He didn't know what she was saying to them other than that it was good news. For them. For him it meant another week of wrestling with demons.

All too aware that this would merely delay the inevitable heartache, he thought maybe they all needed to rip this bandage off and say goodbye today. This very minute.

There was more whispered conversation, but Michael didn't catch it. Nor did he care about it.

He had half a mind to confront her, to boot her out of his house. *Got that?* he thought. *His* house. Not hers. She should have no control over what went on here.

He heard the front door open and close. He

heard the children whispering. He heard her voice, soft and husky now, talking to them.

He tapped his knuckles on the fireplace mantel, working hard to control his anger. Control was paramount. It kept him whole and calm. When he had control, his life made sense.

And suddenly Samantha was behind him. He hadn't heard her enter the room. He sensed her, though. She was there now, not speaking, and barely breathing.

He didn't know how he could be so aware of her, so in tune with her presence. Where this woman was concerned, he was like a divining rod drawn to water.

"Why didn't you give your children a Christmas celebration?" she asked softly.

There was not one ounce of reproach in her voice, but guilt hit him like a sucker punch to the gut. He'd known it wasn't fair, but selfishly he'd wanted to ignore the season. His pain and his grief and his despair had clouded his judgment.

He'd thought his children were young enough not to know the difference or what they were missing. He'd been wrong. So damned wrong.

But he didn't need this woman, this stranger, to rub his face in his failures.

He loved his children and they loved him. Period.

"Would you tell me what happened?" There was a soft plea in her voice. "Please?"

What? Bleed here in front of her? Slit his wrists and expose three years of agony?

He didn't respond.

"Why don't you celebrate Christmas?"

"Let it go," Michael said through a constricted throat.

No Christmas talk. No sorrow. Leave it buried where it belongs.

"Why not celebrate for the children?"

"That's enough," he shouted and stormed from the room.

"Daddy? Daddeeeeee," Lily wailed from the hallway and ran after him. He heard Samantha hushing the child. He hoped she was holding her.

He couldn't. He'd reached his limit. He'd given and given and given of himself until he'd bled. He'd nursed his wife himself. He'd done the foulest jobs because he loved her. He'd held her when she was nothing more than skin and bones. How much was a man supposed to bear, for God's sake?

"Shh. Shh. Everything will be okay."

Even from back here staring out to his yard

and outbuildings, he could hear Samantha's voice and it pained him.

He should be the one comforting his children.

When the children calmed down, Samantha set Lily on her own two feet and stood. "Jason, go to the kitchen and get snacks for you and the children. Ask the younger ones to set the table. Make sure you each get a couple of cookies. Okay?"

"Sure, Mom. Want me to get the rest of the groceries from the truck first?"

She nodded.

Only after all of the children were in the kitchen did Samantha look for Michael. She didn't have to go far.

He stood at the end of the hallway, in the mudroom, at the back door with one hand high on the doorjamb and the other tucked into his pant pocket.

His shoulders were rigid.

He stared outside. What did he see? A winter wonderland? Or was his vision turned inward, to the dark internal hell of his lovely wife's death?

"Are you all right?" she asked quietly. Now that she'd seen the photographs of his wife and witnessed the depth of his love for her, his reactions made sense.

There was only one option now and that was to push through with her plan, but her heart pounded.

"I'm a good father." He sounded belligerent, but also like maybe he was trying to convince himself.

"Yes, you are."

"Don't humor me," he snapped.

She swallowed an exasperated sigh. "I'm not. I mean it. Truly. Your children love you. You love them. Since the moment I arrived, I haven't doubted it. They are your world. In the short time I've been here, I've witnessed how devoted you are to them and how well you take care of them."

She stepped close and settled her hand on his arm.

He jerked away from her. "Don't touch me." Tone harsh, he continued, "Before you came, we were fine. We got along. There was no crying, no shouting. The children were okay."

For a long time, she didn't say a word while debating how to react. Fight or flight? Fight won. She and her brother had missed so much as children. She couldn't let that happen to Mick and Lily. She had so much affection for quirky, funny Mick and sweet, gentle Lily already.

She might have trouble fighting for herself, but not for kids. For the sake of his children, the battle was on.

"You were not fine," she asserted. "You had repressed your grief so badly there was nothing bright about this home. There were no lows, true, but there weren't any highs, either. I'll bet there's been more laughter in this house since I arrived than in all of the past two years. Am I right?"

He turned on her. "No. You're wrong. It's been more than two years. Lillian had cancer for a year before she died. There. Are you satisfied? I've been *repressing* my children for *three* years."

She stared, assessing the depth of Michael's anger, reaching beneath to feel his grief.

Rigid and terrified, he was running on empty. Any minute now he was going to reach his limit. And that would be a damned shame, because he truly was a good father.

She *had* to do something.

"When I was small," she began, hoping this wasn't a mistake, "we had nothing. My parents didn't care. The only one who gave a hoot about me was Travis. He was a good brother. He was my angel.

"Then my dad died and a year later so did Mom. Cancer. Just like Lillian, but Mom lasted only a month, not a full year. But then, Mom had never had much fight in her."

Michael watched her with his dark, inscrutable gaze.

She continued. "We were left alone. The difference was that we were older than Mick and Lily. I was twelve and Travis sixteen, not babies like your kids."

Travis had been her savior, throughout her childhood and after their deaths. Every child needed a savior.

"The effect of my parents' indifference to me and Travis lingers to this day. Your kids need to heal now."

What kind of people would Lily and Mick grow up to be? Decent and salt-of-the-earth like their father? Certainly. Repressed and holding everything in, also like their father? Beyond a shadow of a doubt.

Samantha couldn't let that happen.

Things had to be turned around, and quickly.

"I'm staying another week—"

"I didn't invite you to."

"—and we're having Christmas."

Michael's fists were clenched. She wasn't afraid, certain in her conviction that he wouldn't hurt her. He glared at her over his shoulder, but he didn't contradict her.

The gauntlet had been thrown down. The challenge had been made. Michael could accept or continue to hide away.

Thunderclouds were less intimidating than what seethed on his brow.

"Who do you think you are to make assumptions about my kids and my home? What gives you the right to make *Christmas*?"

"I'm the person who's going to save you from yourself."

He looked like he might throttle her. When he grasped her arms and pulled her against him, she had a moment of fear. Had she gone too far?

But he didn't hurt her. He kissed her, and it was full of fury, unrestrained passion, and so, so much more than Sammy had ever known in a kiss. She leaned into him, tasting his heat and drinking in every drop of his fervor and returning it with her own. More, more, more.

His heat surrounded her, melting her own remembered grief from childhood.

She took and took, craving everything, but he pulled away too soon, breathing hard.

"This isn't over," he ground out.

She wasn't sure what he meant by *this*, but said, "No, it isn't, but now is not the time."

Resistance still seethed in his dark eyes, but some of it had been spent in that kiss.

"Michael, we both know you saved our lives when you let me and my kids stay here, even though you didn't want us to."

He didn't respond. She forged on. "Let me repay you by making Christmas for the children and for *you*."

He still didn't speak, but at least he didn't disagree.

"It will all turn out right. I promise." Sure of her decision, she called out to the kids, "Get your snowsuits and boots. We're going Christmas tree hunting."

She searched Michael's face before pointing a finger at him and saying, "You bring the ax."

Returning to the kitchen, she put away the perishables from the grocery bags on the floor and left the rest for later.

She stopped and touched her lips.

It had been a long time since she'd been kissed like that, with that much pent-up desire. Not since...well, never.

She took a moment to compose herself, drawing on every ounce of strength she possessed to set aside her own needs for the sake of the children. They mattered, not her.

Back in the hallway, she waded into the

chaos of twelve children scrambling into boots, snowsuits, hats and mittens.

"How can only four kids make so much mess?" she wailed, overdoing it for a laugh.

Mick giggled, his relief that she was making light of things palpable.

The other two younger children followed his lead, but not Jason. He watched her and Michael, somber and on guard.

She leaned close and whispered, "Stop worrying."

When he didn't relax, she wrapped her arms around him and lifted him off his feet.

"Mo-o-o-om," he protested, but didn't push her away. She might have only another year or two before he got too cool for hugging, and Samantha planned to get her fill.

When she put him down, he glanced at Michael, apprehension still lingering.

Michael approached and Samantha tensed. She wasn't afraid that he would hurt her, but the wrong words could crush her son.

Michael settled a wide, blunt-fingered hand on Jason's shoulder.

"You want to help me cut down the tree?" He didn't look happy, but his voice was gentle.

"I can help," Jason said with a small smile.

"Okay. Between the two of us, we'll get 'er done."

Michael turned to Samantha, his expression a maelstrom of roiling and unsettled emotions.

She knew how he felt.

"Jason and I will head out to the barn and get what we need. You finish with the little ones," he said, his tone apologetic despite the anger still lurking in his eyes.

They left and Sammy turned her attention to the children, bringing order to the chaos of too many outdoor clothes.

When they stepped outside, they found Michael and Jason talking quietly, Michael holding an ax and a length of rope and Jason gripping a second rope attached to a toboggan.

"A sled," Colt squealed. "Look, Mom. Can I ride on it?"

Without waiting for a response, he ran over and threw himself on it, followed by Mick and Lily.

"I can't pull it with them on it," Jason complained, unhappy that his task had been ruined. "They're too heavy."

"I'll do it." Sammy tried, but the weight was just too much for her.

"Here." Michael handed his rope to Jason. "Carry this."

He handed the ax to Samantha. "Trade you." He relieved her of the toboggan and pulled it out of the yard, making it look easy. "The toboggan will flatten the snow enough for you to walk behind me."

Michael set off across a field, breaking through thigh-high snow that hadn't yet had a chance to harden. Samantha brought up the rear with the ax slung over her shoulder.

Michael tossed back over his shoulder. "Snow's too deep for us to go far. We're only going to that small copse of woods right there."

He pulled up at the edge of the field.

Samantha stared at the trees. "They're too tall."

"These are Colorado spruce. They grow tall. In the woods, though, I'll find us something smaller."

He might have been addressing his comments to her, but he wasn't meeting her eye. "Jason and I will head into the woods. Can you entertain the kids here?"

"I can stay with them."

What was he feeling? Guilt? Shame? He was a hard man to read.

The children tumbled into the snow like a litter of kittens.

Mick showed all of them, including Samantha, how to build a snowman.

"You've done this before," she commented.

Mick grinned. "Dad taught us how."

So, she'd been right earlier. He was a good father, engaged with his children. They hadn't had snowball fights, but they'd built snowmen.

Too bad he couldn't hide his sadness from them.

Lily showed Colt how to make a snow angel.

"I love snow, Mom!"

Ten minutes later, the sound of chopping echoed in the cold air.

"Listen." Samantha clapped her mitten-covered hands. "They found a tree!"

"Yay!" Colt did a backflip in the snow.

"Can we watch?" Mick grasped her hand, a look of pleading on his face.

"I don't see why not."

When the kids started to run in Michael's footsteps for the woods, she yelled, "Stop!"

As one, they turned.

"We have to be careful and go slowly. Until we know exactly where they are and which way the tree is going to fall, we'll keep our distance and call out. Everyone hold hands."

They ventured into the woods single file, with Samantha leading the way.

Michael's solid form came into view.

When Sammy noticed it was Jason wielding the ax, her heart lurched.

Michael saw her and raised a hand. "He's good. I showed him what to do. He's being careful."

The man was closed off, performing all of the right functions and saying all of the right things, but a ghost of himself.

Samantha watched for a few minutes. Jason was being careful. She relaxed. His efforts weren't getting him far, but it was good to see him try. His young, unformed muscles tired soon and Michael took the ax from him, squeezing his shoulder.

"You did well. Step back." When Jason reached the others at the side of the clearing, Michael swung the ax in a powerful arc and put a good-sized dent into the trunk of the tree.

Another few whacks later, Michael pointed to a spot several feet away. "I want everyone over there."

Samantha herded the children over.

Michael swung.

"Timber-r-r," Colt yelled and the tree came down, sending plumes of powdery snow into the air.

The children whooped and jumped, including Jason, all of his earlier wariness gone. He ran across the clearing and around the fallen tree to throw his arms around Michael's waist.

"Awesome!"

Stunned, Michael held his arms out from his sides. A split second later, he dropped the ax and hugged the boy to him.

When he said, "We did good," his voice sounded thick.

Samantha blinked away the tears blurring her vision, the affection between them hurting and warming at the same time.

She and her children would be leaving the ranch. Not until after their February Christmas celebration, but they *would* be leaving.

They had another week to right a wrong, but in that time Jason would idolize Michael even more.

What had Samantha done? Sacrificed her son's future happiness for the sake of Mick and Lily?

Jason had built an attachment to this rock-solid rancher, and why not? Michael had shown him more attention in a handful of days than his own father had in the past five years.

Michael was a natural teacher, made to be a father.

If not for his wife's death, his relationship with his children would have developed unimpeded by grief and anger.

He would have been an amazing father to them.

As it was, the relationship was damaged, but Samantha believed it could be fixed.

With the rope they'd brought along, Michael showed Jason how to secure the tree to the toboggan.

The walk back home took a *lot* longer than the walk over because the little kids had to walk instead of ride.

By the time they arrived at the house, they were fractious and Sammy carried Lily.

Michael and Jason shook as much snow from the tree as they could and stood it up in a corner of the back porch.

"One more thing we have to do, Jason."

Jason hung on Michael's words. "Yeah?"

"Let's head to the barn. We'll dry the ax thoroughly and oil it before we put it away so it won't rust. I'll show you how."

Once the younger children were out of their

clothes, Samantha made hot chocolate and settled them in front of a fire.

"Sammy, I don't got marshmallows."

"I'm afraid we're all out, Lily. I forgot to put them on the list. Drink it as it is, okay?"

"'Kay."

Samantha returned to the kitchen to make chocolate for the adults and Jason. When Michael entered the kitchen, smoothing his hair into place after taking off his hat, he found Sammy with her big purse on the counter.

She handed him a wad of money. "This is for the groceries. The boys and I have eaten you out of house and home."

He tucked his hands into his back pockets.

Samantha frowned. "Please take this."

He shook his head. "Y'all are my guests. I won't take your money."

"We're your unexpected guests and I've just forced myself on you for another week."

"Yeah. Unexpected, true." Still those hands stayed in his pockets. His gaze shifted away, wary and tense. "But you aren't unwelcome. Not completely."

He shot out of the room, trailed by Jason with a satisfied smile warming his features.

Not unwelcome? Her heart warmed. What a shift from just a couple of hours ago. Then she recognized the qualifier. *Not completely.*

She didn't care about his anger or misgivings or…whatever. She was doing the right thing.

Warmed through, she started cooking.

They had a simple dinner that night, with an early bedtime, in beds this time now that they didn't have to sleep in front of the fire.

In the middle of the night, Samantha awoke to find that Lily had joined her and the boys again.

She cuddled the girl close and went back to sleep.

After breakfast, she asked Michael to head back into town with a different kind of shopping list.

"Okay."

"Can I come?" Jason asked.

"Sure."

Again, Michael refused to take her money.

Sammy put her wallet away. Stubborn man. She had the satisfaction of knowing he would be shocked at some of the items on her list.

She also knew he would move heaven and earth to find every single one.

After they left, she gathered the little ones close.

She wouldn't use old Christmas ornaments. She didn't even bother to look through the house for any. Michael was too fragile for that. He would be devastated to be faced with Christmas the way he and his wife had shared it.

Samantha had to forge new traditions until Michael was healed enough to accept the old again.

When Michael and Jason returned, Samantha outlined everything they would be doing to celebrate Christmas in February.

"Christmas what?" Mick asked.

"I'm calling it Christmas in February."

"I never heard of that."

"Me, neither," said Colt.

"I made it up," she responded.

She turned to Michael. "I'll need you and Jason to put up the tree today. The rest of us will start on making decorations."

Jason followed Michael. Between the two of them, they erected it in the corner.

On Michael's large harvest table, she spread an old tablecloth with one hole in it. She'd found it in the bottom of the drawer that held place mats, napkins and good tablecloths.

She cut out strips of the colored construction paper Michael had picked up for her.

Setting out pots of glue, she had the children make paper chains.

After instructing them carefully, she went into the living room to glimpse the tree.

Michael had chosen well. Even without decorations, it added a festive note to the room, including the odd but refreshing scent of evergreen.

Rummaging through the bags, she pulled out the strings of small white lights she'd ordered.

Michael didn't look happy. In fact, there was pain in the depths of his eyes, but he did everything she asked him to do.

The woman asked a lot of him.

Michael took the lights from her and unraveled them. He taught Jason how to string them properly, hiding the wires in the branches, but twisting and positioning the lights so they showed to advantage.

How many times had he done this in his married life?

Every movement, every remembered motion, evoked Lillian.

Samantha, this stranger, wanted him to forget his wife, forget that their life together had ever happened and that her death mattered.

He knew that was unfair, but it was how it *felt.*

Michael hated feeling emotions, all except

for anger, and that served an essential purpose. Sometimes it was all that kept him putting one foot in front of the other.

If he let go of his anger, what would be left? Grief. Immense, overwhelming grief.

His anger had at least kept a portion of that at bay.

And once he'd dealt with his grief? What then? What part would Lillian, his first love, his only love, have in his life?

She would be gone for good.

He would have to face the final, irrevocable loss and accept that Lillian would never, ever come back.

His hands shook only a little while he strung lights, but it was an effort to keep them still. What this woman was doing wasn't right—not for him—but so damned good for his children.

Their bright chatter in the kitchen, their happiness, spread to every corner of his house.

And so, he did whatever he was told.

Which was how he found himself on the sofa hours later stringing popcorn and fresh cranberries to make garlands for the tree.

Long-suffering Jason sat beside him doing the same thing while Samantha helped the little ones put the paper chains on the tree.

Michael and Jason had been given this chore because the smaller kids had done nothing but eat the popcorn. Plus the only needles they'd been allowed to use, thick and dull needles, had cracked too many kernels.

Glancing around the room, Michael noticed that the order Samantha had imposed after her arrival had descended into chaos once again.

This was different, though, new and fresh and happy. Not out of control like a house that had given up on itself.

They settled into bed that night and the kids fell asleep hard, while Michael lay on the sofa staring at the Christmas tree and wished they were all back in the living room with him.

Funny that no one had complained about his snoring while in the big room, but his kids still didn't want him to share their small bedrooms.

They'd turned on the Christmas lights earlier in the evening and Michael hadn't yet extinguished them.

He was afraid to, because the dark edges of his grief hovered and bedeviled and threatened to overwhelm him.

Chapter 11

The next morning, Samantha asked Michael if she could borrow his truck.

He handed her the keys.

Considering his children's excitement, how they'd insisted on eating breakfast in the living room in front of the lighted tree, he could deny her nothing.

"We're going Christmas shopping. I'm taking the little ones, okay?"

He nodded.

Half an hour later, Michael stood alone in his living room and turned in a circle.

It didn't feel right, to be in this empty house by himself.

He remembered the night they'd come and how he'd hated their arrival.

Now he couldn't wait for them to return.

He headed out the back door to spend time with his animals.

As well, Samantha had said they were going Christmas shopping. He had some ideas of his own.

He might not like this idea of Christmas in February, but— Whoa. That wasn't accurate. It wasn't that he didn't like it. He just didn't know if he could survive it.

Samantha held Lily's hand while they walked down Main Street.

The two younger boys ran ahead and Jason stayed close to her, by her side.

"Here," Lily said, pointing to the door of the hardware store they'd just come to. "Daddy likes this store."

"Boys," she called, and Colt and Mick ran back to join them. "We're going in here."

Once inside, she asked Mick and Lily, "What kinds of things does your dad like?"

"Old stuff," Mick said in a normal tone. Sammy smiled. He'd remembered his hearing aids.

Samantha grinned. "Yes. I've noticed that. What else does he like? Lily? Any ideas?"

The little girl nodded. "Come." She took Samantha's hand and dragged her toward the back of the store. There, past nails and screws, hammers and drills, and an assortment of tools Sammy couldn't begin to name, was a wall full of old tools. Ancient things. Again, she couldn't have named them.

They were pricey, as though the town either wanted or needed to sell its heritage, but couldn't manage to actually part with it.

They might have been cleared out of barns and basements, but someone knew their value as pieces of the town's history.

Her mind ran through her budget for the month. Michael hadn't let her pay for their food, but at least had eventually taken money for the Christmas items she'd wanted, after some persuasion.

She was okay for the rest of the month, but she certainly couldn't purchase many of these items.

"Which one do you like?" She leaned down toward Lily. "Which do you think your daddy will like?"

She held her breath. *Please don't pick anything too expensive.*

Lily stuck out one tiny finger from her tiny square fist, surprisingly like her father's, and touched a wooden ruler.

"That? He'd like that?" There was something wrong with it. "Why doesn't it have all of the numbers? It starts at twenty and ends at twenty-six. Then there's ten to sixteen upside down on top of those. Very strange." At one end an odd brass hinge had a circle shape jutting from it away from the ruler.

"I'll show you." Lily's soft voice cut through the boys' chatter.

She picked up the ruler and separated the top section from the bottom along the circle. She lifted a piece of wood from behind the ruler on one side, and then lifted another on the other end using a second hinge. The she opened the entire thing from a center brass hinge.

"See?" She giggled. "It's long!"

A wooden yardstick that folded and unfolded, it clearly delighted Lily. Samantha wasn't sure whether the child wanted it for herself or for her father.

"See?" Lily set the tip of her finger on a minuscule spike of brass sticking out from the top of the ruler and pointed to a hole farther along. "This goes into here."

"Ingenious." She studied the child as she opened and closed the yardstick again. "Would your daddy like it?"

Lily nodded so hard her hat fell sideways.

Samantha adjusted it and said, "Then we'll buy it for him."

The ruler had seen a lot of years and a lot of use. It was nicked and a little dirty, but Lily loved it. She insisted on carrying it to the cash desk.

There, Samantha asked the clerk for brass cleaner and advice on polishing the ruler.

Lily tried to climb the counter to watch the transaction and Sammy picked her up.

On her other side, Jason leaned against her and said, "Can cleaning it be my part of the Christmas present?"

Samantha ran her fingers through his hair. "What a great idea. Michael would really like that."

She paid and they left.

Farther down Main Street, they came to a diner. "Let's have lunch."

She stepped inside, into a time warp of red vinyl and gray linoleum.

They took a table at the window. The waitress came over, a throwback to the fifties with her red-and-white polka-dot dress and white knit shrug. Full-figured, she did the fitted bodice and tight waist justice. An impressive set of hips made the dress flare dramatically.

The woman stared at Samantha curiously.

"Vy, hi!" Lily said. "It's me! Lily!"

"I see you there, Miss Lily. You, too, Mick. Your dad not with you today?"

"He's at home doing chores," Mick said. "We're Christmas shopping."

She glanced at Samantha. "New friends *and* Christmas shopping. Curiouser and curiouser." She delighted Sammy by quoting *Alice's Adventures in Wonderland*, Samantha's all-time favorite story.

"I'm Samantha Read." She stuck out her hand and the waitress, Vy, gave it a surprisingly firm shake.

"Travis's sister?"

"Yes. These are my children, Jason and Colt."

"I'm Violet Summer, but everyone calls me Vy. Jason, Colt and I have met." She smiled at them. "What's this about Christmas shopping?"

"We're going to have Christmas in February."

"Not just Christmas shopping, but actually having Christmas? In February?"

Samantha stood up and drew Vy aside. "It turns out the children haven't celebrated Christmas since their mother died. I'm giving them Christmas now."

Vy brightened. "Love it."

"May I ask to leave the children here to eat

while I run out to pick up gifts for them? I'd rather their presents remain a surprise until Christmas morning. *Our* Christmas morning."

"For such a worthy cause, I would watch them, but I'm run off my feet. I'm sure Rachel would do it for you, though."

"Rachel?"

Vy cocked her head. Her gaze became speculative. "Rachel McGuire. You don't know about Rachel?"

"I know who she is, but I haven't had a chance to meet her yet."

"She's in the booth in the window on the other side of the door. I can take the children's orders while you talk to her."

As Samantha stepped away Mick burst out with, "Cherry cola!" and turned back.

Vy waved her hand. "I got this. Mick, you know your dad will only let you have a little bit of pop. I'll split a small one between you and Lily."

Colt looked imploringly toward Samantha. "Vy, can you do the same for Colt and Jason?" she asked. "Split one and only one?"

"No problem. Okay, kids, let's talk about food." With one hand, Vy gently urged Samantha away. "I can handle the children. I'll make sure they eat healthy food."

While all four children tried to order at once, and Vy laughed, Samantha approached the other table slowly. She wanted to meet the woman who had finally snagged Travis's affection, but what if they didn't like each other?

There were four women chatting amiably in the booth, the bond of friendship evident even to a stranger. She stood at the end of the table. As one, they stopped talking and looked up at her.

The woman closest to her stared and then broke into the sunniest grin. She stood up and held out her hand. "You must be Samantha. Travis has told me so much about you."

"He has?"

"Oh, yes. I'm Rachel and I'm so happy to finally meet you."

Samantha took her hand and shook it. "Please call me Sammy."

"I'm Travis's…um…"

"Oh, for God's sake, Rachel, just say it," one of the women said. "You're his girlfriend."

"His fiancée," another said.

Samantha studied the young woman critically. Her brother deserved the absolute, utter best.

Rachel's smile faltered.

She wasn't beautiful, but attractive. Thick tawny hair framed a face dominated by hazel eyes. Some of the golden streaks in her hair matched highlights in her eyes.

In the depths of those eyes, Samantha saw what had been missing in Travis's life. Goodness. Kindness. A steady temperament. And a smile that could light up a baseball stadium.

Samantha threw her arms around Rachel, whispering, "Thank you. Thank you."

She drew back, but kept her hands on the other woman's arms. "Thank you for making him happy. Travis is— Travis deserves—" She didn't have the words.

"I know," Rachel said. "He's the best."

"Don't—" *Don't hurt him*, she'd been about to say, but stopped herself. She didn't want to offend.

"I won't," Rachel responded as though she'd understood. "If I were his sister, I'd be concerned about a stranger stepping in, too. Please don't worry. I couldn't possibly love him more."

Samantha's eyes misted. Discreetly, she turned away and dabbed at her eyes.

"I'd like to get to know you better."

"And you, too. In the meantime, I'm here on a mission. I need to ask you to babysit both my two children and Michael Moreno's two. I know this is presumptuous, but—"

Rachel's face lit up. "Your boys are here? Where? I'd love to meet them. Travis talks about them nonstop. He misses them."

They turned to leave, but a woman with amazing blond curls stopped her. "Rach, before you go, can you introduce us?"

"Cripes, where are my manners? Samantha, this is Honey Armstrong, Nadine Campbell and Max Porter."

Honey was the woman with the curls, almost doll-like with deep-set blue eyes, a fair complexion and full lips.

Nadine had long red hair as straight as though she'd ironed it. The red was real, Samantha was certain, because of the woman's paler-than-pale skin. She'd darkened her lashes to black and had used a pale mauve shadow to highlight a fine pair of green eyes.

She looked vaguely familiar, but Samantha couldn't place her. Interesting.

By comparison, the woman who sat on her far side, Max, looked like a boy. Plain and simple, there was no better way to put it.

Her short, dark, roughly cropped hair appeared to have been combed with her fingers. It probably hadn't seen a brush in years. An oversize plaid flannel shirt, over a waffle-weave undershirt that peeked out at the neckline, hid any womanly assets she might possess.

A smattering of freckles across her nose softened her look. She might have a pretty face, as gamine and heart-shaped as it was, but for her sullen expression, her demeanor a sharp contrast to her friends.

Samantha shook hands with all of them then turned back to Rachel. "I wouldn't ordinarily leave the children like this, but I'm shopping for Christmas presents for them and don't want them to see what I'm buying."

"Wow, that's early," Honey said. "I think I'm organized, but shopping for next Christmas in February is brilliant. There should be good sales."

"No. Not for next Christmas. For the one that's just past." She explained what she was doing and was met with wide approval.

Nadine said, "Now *that's* brilliant, and truly kind. I like it."

Samantha led Rachel to her table. They got there just as Vy arrived with a tray of small fruit juice glasses filled with dark liquid. A slice of pineapple sat on the lip of each glass. It looked like Vy had snipped straws in half to accommodate the short glasses.

"This is all the pop you're getting today, so

sip it slowly. I want everyone eating the pineapple, too. It's good for you."

She passed the glasses around and the children started to drink right away. "You'll all have milk with your lunches."

"Mick and Lily, you know Rachel McGuire?" Sammy asked.

They waved and chorused, "Hi, Rachel."

"Jason and Colt, this is Rachel. She knows your uncle Travis. She's going to sit with you while I shop for a bit."

Rachel slid into the booth beside Lily and wiped a dribble of cola from the child's chin.

"I'll be quick. Lunch is on me. Please order whatever you like," Samantha said.

"I'm stuffed. I already ate with the girls. Go do your thing and don't worry. The children and I will get along just fine."

Samantha knew there was a large new shopping mall up the highway, but she chose to stay on Main Street. She wanted to get to know this town and its people.

She needed to get a handle on why Travis had chosen this place to be their home.

Halfway down the block, she found an old toy store, with a window display that looked like it hadn't changed in thirty years. The interior, though, was a delight, with every kind of jigsaw puzzle ever invented, old-fashioned mechanical building sets, every toy imaginable and an impressive display of dolls.

Samantha wanted to replace that raggedy old doll of Lily's. The more she studied the dolls in the shop, the harder it was to choose. She imagined buying one of these beauties, but all that came to mind, incongruously, was a look of betrayal on Lily's face when she opened a new doll, as though Samantha had told her that Puff wasn't good enough.

Although she looked around, nothing else hit her as just right for Lily.

For Mick, she bought a 100-piece bucket of Meccano pieces. For Colt, she picked out an advance toolbox of Meccano pieces. They'd both been gung ho about Michael's old tools. Between the two of them, the boys could build amazing things.

Jason had a different character altogether. He wasn't a builder so much as a tender. He loved taking care of creatures. He loved animals.

She chose a 1,000-piece jigsaw puzzle, a gorgeous panorama of a ranch with horses in the fields and a rancher who looked vaguely like Michael. If she secretly hoped that Michael would do the puzzle with Jason, she could be forgiven for dreaming.

On impulse, she picked up a pot of puzzle

glue, in case Jason wanted to keep the puzzle as a reminder of an idyllic couple of weeks spent on Michael's ranch.

At the cash register, she paid and asked, "Is there somewhere in town where I can buy fabric?"

"Sophie at the department store carries some. Or you can drive out to the new mall."

Samantha sensed a test here, but the salesman smiled pleasantly. "No, I'd rather shop in town."

That earned her a big smile and a heartfelt *thank you* when she walked out of the store.

At the department store, she checked out the small fabric section and found colorful remnants she could use to make Puff some new clothes for Lily's Christmas present.

On the way to cash out, a pile of brightly colored fabrics caught her eye—velvets and brocades in Christmas fabrics. They were marked down because, of course, it was after Christmas.

They were fabrics meant to make table runners and festive placemats, but Samantha bought red fabric with small gold poinsettias for a skirt for Lily to wear on Christmas-in-February Day.

She also bought white Swiss eyelet to make a blouse.

On impulse, she picked up huge bulk skeins of yarn to make mittens for all the boys. It was only acrylic, but the boys wouldn't care. For Michael, she picked up dark gray wool and a pattern for a hat with a thick, ribbed border.

Certifiably crazy for expecting to be able to get all of this done in a week, she nonetheless walked out of the store wearing a huge grin.

Forty-five minutes later, she returned to the diner, priding herself on finding everything so quickly.

The front booth was empty. Spinning around, she searched the diner for her children. Gone.

Heart pounding, she raced to the counter.

Sure, Manny d'Onofrio had said that he'd called off his dogs, but Samantha doubted she would ever fully relax again.

Vy came around the counter, saying, "Hey, it's okay. Rachel and the girls took them to the park. They finished their lunches and got restless."

"Oh." The sudden absence of fear left her deflated. "Where is the park?"

"At the opposite end of town. Turn left when you leave here."

"Okay. First, I'll settle the bill."

"Already done. The girls put their money together and paid."

"But—"

"Don't worry. They were happy to do it. Every one of them loves children." Vy carried a coffeepot to a table and refilled cups. "By the way, your boys are adorable. So polite."

"Thank you," Samantha responded faintly, overwhelmed by the warmth of these women. Of this place. Maybe Travis had been right about Rodeo.

Vy studied her. "You planning to stay around?"

Samantha nodded.

"What kind of skills do you have?"

"Skills?" Strange question. "Why do you ask?"

Vy laughed. "No need to look so suspicious. I phrased it wrong. The girls and I are trying to resurrect the town's old amusement park for next summer." She returned the pot to the burner.

"Why?"

Vy looked at her blankly. "Why what?"

"Why are you resurrecting an old amusement park?"

"We need to do something to save the town. It's a great place to live and we love it here, but businesses and ranches are failing.

We have no manufacturing. No industry." She wiped the already-clean counter. "But what if we could bring in tourist dollars every summer? What if we could convince our young people to stay by giving them jobs, especially if we could lengthen the season?"

She took a lungful of air. "Sorry. That was quite a speech, wasn't it? It's just that we get excited when we think about it. We might be able to pull it off. To actually save our town."

Samantha smiled. "I admire your passion."

"You hungry?" Vy asked.

"Starving."

"I'll pack up a lunch to go. Take it with you to the park."

Sammy ordered from the menu then said, "I'm an accountant."

Vy's eyes widened and she whispered, "Perfect."

"Why?"

"We don't have anyone to make an operating budget for us and set up ticket sales and take care of money."

"I don't know… I guess I can take a look at what you have planned."

Vy put a brown paper bag on the counter. "Go ask Rachel about it. She'll talk your ear off."

Samantha paid for her lunch and walked

to the park where she found everyone, adults and children, involved in a snowball fight.

She brushed snow from a bench and sat down to eat. Inside the diner lunch bag, she found her sandwich wrapped in waxed paper held closed by a rubber band. Totally retro.

The sandwich, on the other hand, was so cutting-edge it was almost California personified. Avocado, sprouts, goat cheese with pepper and cranberries and some kind of mild aioli were wedged between thick slices of an excellent rosemary focaccia that tasted like it had been grilled in olive oil. The entire thing had been toasted so the cheese melted.

Lily ran over and sat beside her. "Did you get presents, Sammy?"

"Yep, but that's all I'm saying about that. You can stick me with hot pokers, but I won't tell you what I bought for you."

Lily giggled.

"You'll have to wait until Christmas-in-February morning. Okay?"

"'Kay." A small frown furrowed her brow. "Did you buy your own present?"

"No."

"Who will buy it? We gotted Daddy's and you gotted ours, but no one gotted yours."

Samantha shrugged. "It's okay. It doesn't matter."

Lily's mouth drooped and her eyes filled.

Samantha cast about for a quick distraction. "What did you have for lunch?"

"I had a slider and roasted potatoes. Vy made me have two slices of cucumber, too. I eated it all."

"I ate it all," Samantha corrected automatically.

"No, you didn't, Sammy. I did!"

Samantha burst out laughing. This town was good for her.

Smart Vy for serving the child one slider instead of a whole large burger.

"I drinked my milk, too."

Sammy didn't make the mistake of trying to correct her grammar again.

"What's those red things in your sammich?"

"Cranberries. These are sweetened, though, not like the fresh ones we used for the tree. Try one."

She fed Lily a dried cranberry. "It's good, Sammy. I like it."

"Do you want more?"

"No. I have to go play." She ran off, falling down and tumbling in the snow. She picked herself up and kept on running.

Rachel joined Samantha on the bench.

"Vy told me to ask you about the amusement park."

Rachel glowed like the Christmas tree they'd all just decorated at Michael's house.

"It's old. It's been on the outskirts of town for almost a century. The town is named after the rodeo that was part of the annual fair." Rachel turned to face Samantha. "The owner grew too old to keep it going every year. He retired fifteen years ago and it's been down since then. We want to bring it back, to make it a paying venture. This town needs it, to provide jobs and keep our youth here."

"Wonderful goals. Who exactly are *we*?"

"Nadine, Honey, Violet, Maxine and me."

"Vy mentioned that you need someone to handle the money. I'm an accountant."

"Yes. Travis told me. I was hoping to convince you to volunteer your time. We can't pay you. Not this year, anyway. Not until we see whether the fair makes any money."

"Did Travis also tell you about the problems I had with my former boss?" Might as well get it out in the open.

Rachel frowned. "He said you testified against him and he went to jail. Travis's old girlfriend came to town and said his men were coming here. Travis also said everything's all right now."

"Yes. Manny backed off and called off his men. He's gone through quite a change. He's become religious."

Rachel's skepticism showed. "Do you believe him? Can people really change that much?"

"I believe him, yes. His letter was more heartfelt than anything I ever read from Manny in the past."

"Why did you bring this up?"

"I wanted to gauge your reaction. See if you thought I had anything to do with Manny's extortion."

"Did you?"

"No."

Rachel smiled, bringing out the sun. "That's good enough for me. If you don't mind brutally long hours for no money whatsoever, you are now a member of the Rodeo Amusement Park and Fair Revival Committee."

Samantha laughed. "How can I resist such a generous offer? I'll give you whatever time I can spare once I start work."

Rachel stood. "I have to tell the others."

Samantha finished her sandwich and packed up her garbage.

When she heard a lot of squealing, she

glanced up. All of the women converged on her, chattering and asking her questions.

It seemed that even before she'd moved into her new home with Travis, she was already part of this town.

Jason approached solemnly, with Lily by his side.

"Mom, can I have twenty dollars?"

"May I have twenty dollars?"

Jason frowned. "No, Mom. I'm asking *you* for it."

Samantha laughed. It seemed that grammar lessons didn't work on older children, either.

"Why do you need the money?" she asked.

"I can't tell you."

"It's a secret, Sammy," Lily said. "You aren't supposed to know we're going shopping for you."

Jason glanced down at the girl, his expression part frustration and part affection. He sighed. "Pretend you didn't hear that part, Mom."

"I can do that." She opened her purse and took out a twenty-dollar bill. "Call the boys and let's go. You and Lily can shop and then we'll head back to the ranch."

Minutes later, they were on Main Street, waiting outside a small gift shop while Jason and Lily browsed inside.

"Are you two cold?" she asked Mick and Colt.

"Only a little, Mom. Can we have hot chocolate when we get home?"

"Sure, Colt. How about you, Mick? Hot chocolate for you, too?"

Jason and Lily emerged from the gift shop, grinning. Jason carried a small bag. "We can go now, Mom."

"Okay, everyone into the car. We did good work today, kids. We're going to celebrate with hot chocolate and cookies when we get home."

The kids cheered and Samantha drove back to the ranch. When she turned onto Michael's land, the unique, unsettling feeling of coming home flooded her.

She followed the chattering children into the house, with Lily sound asleep in her arms.

Inside it was toasty warm and smelled like simmering beef.

The boys took off their boots and raced to hang up their outdoor clothes in the mudroom.

Michael emerged from the kitchen, wiping his big hands on a tea towel. A small smiled hovered at the corners of his mouth. Was he glad they were all home?

"You buy out the town?" he asked.

"I was good. I found some bargains." She smiled. "Take Lily, will you? She's tiny, but..."

"She's heavier than she looks." Michael returned her smile and took his sleeping daughter from her arms. He deposited her on the sofa, eased her out of her winter clothes and covered her with an afghan.

He might not be happy about Christmas in February, but she thought he liked the happiness on the children's faces.

"I promised everyone hot chocolate and cookies." She hung up her coat and slipped out of her boots. "Oh, Michael, they were so good. Full of beans, sure, but such caring children. We've each done a good job with them, haven't we?"

"I like to think so." His smile dimmed, and she realized her making Christmas for them implied disapproval of how he was raising his children.

"*We* have." She passed him in the hallway on her way to put on milk to heat up. He smelled like fried onions. "What are you making?"

"Stew. I didn't know anything vegetarian to make for you."

"I picked up frozen spinach and some feta in town. I'll make myself an omelet." She snapped her fingers. "Shoot. I was carrying Lily and forgot to bring in the packages."

"I'll get them."

She nodded and went to the kitchen.

Minutes later, she heard him return and realized he might be able to see his gift.

She rushed to the hallway, but all of the bags had their tops folded down.

He looked curious, but didn't ask to see anything. She needed this man on her side and fully committed to this if the children were going to be happy.

"Do you want to see what I bought for the children?"

He shrugged indifference, but a tiny sparkle in his eye betrayed him. He might be upset with her for forcing Christmas on him, but maybe he'd missed it just a little.

"Follow me." She turned down the heat under the milk and led him to his bedroom, closing the door behind him.

"Just a sec." She dropped the bags onto his bed and, with her back to him, rummaged through them until she found his ruler and the yarn to make his hat. She put those into their own bag and rolled the top down. "Excuse me for a second. I'll be right back."

After leaving the bag in Lily's room, she returned to Michael's bedroom.

"Mom, we're hungry," Colt called from the playroom.

"I'll be there in a minute."

She closed the door and pulled everything out of the bags and explained what was for each child. She looked at him with expectant eyes. "What do you think?"

He picked up the jigsaw puzzle first and ran his finger over one of the horses. "This looks like Rascal."

"Does it? I think Jason will like it a lot."

"I think he will, too." He put it down and picked up the Meccano sets. "These are great. Look, you can make a tractor."

"I know. The boys are going to have so much fun." She picked up the fabric for Lily's skirt. "It's pretty, isn't it? I think Lily will like that it's sparkly. I know it's meant for place mats and that sort of thing, but Lily won't know that. She'll only be wearing it for one day, anyway."

"I guess. I don't know anything about fabric."

"Can you get me one of her dresses or skirts so I can use it as a pattern? The shop didn't have any."

Michael shuffled his feet, but didn't respond or head for the door.

She glanced up. "What?"

"I, um, I've never bought her a dress."

"Oh, dear. I'll have to take measurements. She'll wonder why. It might spoil the surprise." She tapped her finger against her lips. "I'll have to find a creative way to figure it out."

"What's all of this for?" He picked up one of the bargain skeins of yarn.

"I'm knitting the boys mittens."

Michael nodded. "Good idea. I know Mick can wear out a pair in half a season." He seemed to be coming around and maybe getting into the spirit a bit.

She packed the presents back into their bags.

"Let's make the kids a snack." He left the room and Sammy placed the bags on the floor of Michael's closet.

She retrieved the bag with Michael's present and hid that one in his closet, too.

In the kitchen, Michael was already getting cheese and apples ready.

Samantha made hot chocolate and called the boys.

In the living room, Lily let out a wail. Michael went to her and carried her into the kitchen.

"Where was everybody?" the sleepy girl asked from her father's shoulder.

"The boys were playing. Sammy and I were making snacks." Michael rested his head on top of Lily's. "You hungry?"

Lily giggled. "You sound rumbly again, Daddy."

"I always do." He kissed her forehead. "You want to sit by yourself or stay with me and listen to me rumble while you eat?"

"Rumble."

Michael sat and settled his daughter onto his lap.

Samantha put a small hot chocolate on the table in front of him. "That's Lily's."

He picked up the miniature mug with the bunny rabbits on the side and said, "I figured as much." Then he lifted his pinky and mimed drinking from the tiny cup. The kids broke up.

Amid the laughter, Sammy marveled. Despite his grumpiness, he really was a kind man.

Chapter 12

Christmas-in-February preparations filled the following week.

While Michael and Jason spent long hours tending to the cattle, the younger children did as they were told by Samantha.

Today's assignment, apparently, was baking and decorating gingerbread houses.

The boys had already finished theirs and were playing on the veranda.

Jason and Michael stepped through the back door into a spicy wonderland. He toed out of his boots and took off his jacket.

Lily and Samantha murmured in the kitchen while they put the finishing touches on their houses.

Michael did whatever Samantha and the children asked of him, but sometimes wandered his home wondering where all of this whirlwind had come from. How had it happened?

Less than two weeks ago, he'd been living a life of peace, half-dead, yeah, but quiet. And now—

A high-pitched scream from the kitchen cut through the silence.

Lily!

Michael launched himself down the hallway, his mind crowded with ugly possibilities. Had she burned herself? Been cut?

He raced around the corner and through the doorway.

Lily stood on the far side of the kitchen, Samantha crouching by her side. When Lily saw him, she burst around the table and launched herself into his arms.

Only once she was there did her smile register with him.

Relief gusted out of him. She wasn't hurt.

What would he have done if—? How could he cope were she—? It didn't bear thinking about.

"Daddy! Daddy! We made a happy house." Her smile beamed on him like summer sunshine.

What was she talking about?

She wriggled to be put down. He let her go. She grabbed his hand and dragged him around the table where Samantha still crouched.

"Come down here, Daddy, beside me," Lily ordered, animated and happy. "Look!"

Michael crouched beside his daughter. On one wall of a messily decorated house was a smiley face piped on with white icing.

Candies, pretzels and licorice he'd picked up in town covered the rest of the house, but on this one end of the house just the smiley face stood out against the brown gingerbread.

Lily rested her head on his shoulder. "Sammy made me a happy house."

His heart thumped. Talk about symbolism. He inhaled shakily. She had indeed done that, and he didn't mean the tiny house on the table.

Across the top of Lily's head, Michael met Samantha's beautiful blue gaze.

"Yes, Sammy made a happy house." How could he ever thank her? There weren't enough words.

He stood, lifting his daughter with him. He brought Lily's face level with his. Looking at her, he saw bits and pieces of her mother. Lillian shone through in her soft gray eyes and pretty mouth—a blessing and a curse for Michael. Lillian would live on through their daughter. Michael would feel the pain and the joy of his loss every time he looked at her.

Perhaps in time, he would be able to see it without the burden of grief, and instead with gratitude that Lillian had walked this earth, had graced him with her love and had given him two beautiful children.

He kissed Lily's smooth forehead and settled her in his arms.

"I love you, baby."

"Love you, too, Daddy."

"You did an amazing job on your happy house."

Samantha had stood when he had. Lily snagged an arm around her neck and pulled her close.

"Sammy and me both made the happy house. Kiss her, too."

Samantha watched him with wide eyes and parted lips.

The air between them hummed with warmth and possibility.

Michael leaned toward her. She closed her eyes. He touched her forehead with his lips, a meager kiss, but he felt the magic of it to his toes.

"Good job, Daddy," Lily whispered. "We're all friends. Put me down. I have to play."

She ran out of the kitchen while Michael stared at Sammy with his heart doing a crazy dance.

A great chasm opened in front of him and he felt himself falling, hurtling forward before he knew he even wanted to.

His mind could only follow where his heart had already gone.

Lightning did strike twice. Hallelujah. He'd fallen in love with this glorious woman who had indeed made him and his children a happy house.

He had a choice. He could step out into thin air and hope it all worked out, or he could hide away as he'd done for two years.

He knew what Lillian would say. *Go for it, Michael. Wake up. Seize life and love with both hands. We loved each other. I want you to have that again.*

Samantha sidled away, chattering while she cleared the table. Dazed, Michael couldn't follow it. Or maybe Sammy wasn't making sense. She was nervous about something.

Was it him? Did she sense the shift, too?

At the counter, she gathered soiled plastic plates and cups, but her hands shook and knocked over the neat piles she was trying to make.

It seemed that all he'd done since she arrived was take from her. Maybe he could do something for her. He could put her at ease, calm her, gentle her as he would a frightened horse.

Michael approached and placed his hands on the counter on either side of her. He snuggled against her.

She startled, but he said, "Hush. Be still. Please. Just for a moment."

He breathed in her feminine warmth and light perfume. His cheek touched her hair and found it as soft and silken as he had imagined.

"You don't have to be nervous with me. I will never hurt you."

"It's not you. It's change and loneliness and terror of the darkness and silence. I've never had a good relationship. I'm afraid, Michael. Afraid to try again. Afraid to hope."

"Me, too."

His voice seemed to calm her so he talked. He, a man who strung barely four sentences together on any given day, soothed her with whatever came to mind.

In time, she quieted, but her breathing sounded ragged. He knew how she felt. This crazy new mess of emotions set his stomach churning. He wasn't sure what he was doing, or where this was going. He only knew that he needed to hold her.

He brushed his lips along the side of her neck. She dropped her head back onto his chest. Her trust humbled him. He drew his mouth along the smooth satin of her skin by her ear.

"Thank you," he whispered. "For everything."

With the lightest touch, she caressed the length of his arms.

"Oh, Michael. You have no idea how good this is, to have my children in this house where they're treated with respect and affection. Where they're given attention."

Had her husband ignored the kids? Or had it been worse? Had he hurt them? And Samantha, too?

"And having your children to coddle and make happy," she continued, "makes me happy."

"You do. Make them happy, I mean."

He eased back and turned her in his arms.

"You make me happy, too."

"I do?" She sounded breathless. He knew how she felt. He might as well have just run a marathon.

Placing her hands on his chest, she said. "It's good to touch and to be held."

The front door burst open, startling them, and the children ran into the house.

Michael sprang away from Samantha, uncertain whether the interruption had been salvation or damnation.

That night, while Lily slept, Samantha wrestled with her. She had hoped to steal Puff to take measurements, but Lily had a tight enough grip on the doll that Sammy was afraid she would hurt her if she tried to pry the doll away.

She uttered a groan of frustration.

"What's up?" Michael stood in the doorway, watching her.

"I can't get Puff away from her," she whispered. "I need to figure what size to make the doll's clothes."

"Let me."

He tried as well, but Lily stirred and muttered, "Leave me 'lone, Daddy. Tired."

He stood with his hands on his hips. "What do we do?"

Samantha liked the sound of that *we*. All day, she'd tried not to think about the incident in the kitchen. She'd failed.

Every time Michael had stepped close to

her while they'd made dinner, or later when they'd lined the living room windowsills with the gingerbread houses, she'd been intensely aware of him.

Now she scooted past him out of the bedroom and to his room. She stood in the doorway.

"Sometime tomorrow, take her outside to play. The boys, too. I'll stay inside and make clothes and knit mittens."

"Sounds good."

They stared at each other, the air swollen with their unspoken desires, gripped by the struggle between wanting and resisting.

Samantha swayed toward him, but resistance won out.

Without a word, she closed the door and crawled into his big, empty bed.

This week, her sons had moved into Mick's room. The first night had been a nightmare. The boys hadn't fallen asleep for hours, giggling and talking until all hours, but the novelty had worn off and tonight they were quiet.

Samantha lay awake for a long time, not knowing what was the right thing to do, and what was wrong.

Michael watched the children play in the snow while Samantha started making the clothes, distracted by what had happened in the kitchen yesterday and what had almost happened last night in the hallway.

He needed a compass, a map, but had nothing.

Where were the maps for navigating new attraction? For figuring out what to do with a woman who challenged him, but who also made his life infinitely better?

She pushed him beyond his comfortable limits, the narrow boundaries he'd put into place to handle a grief—and anger—that had felt out of control.

He hadn't realized until now how good her pushing had been for him.

Forget about how much his children had benefited. That was amazing. He'd already thanked her for what she had done for them.

He hadn't thought until now what her presence had meant to him, and her looming departure now felt…catastrophic.

He was lost.

On Christmas-in-February Eve, Samantha and Michael hung up the stockings she'd bought on sale.

She studied the room, and every cheap, discounted and homemade decoration they'd used, and she was proud of the results.

"We did well," she whispered, even though the children were down the hallway and fast asleep. Or maybe they weren't. They'd been ridiculously excited about tomorrow morning, especially Mick and Lily.

"*You* did well." He hovered near her, heat shimmering from him and mingling with the flame of the fireplace. She felt it like a caress.

He grasped her arm and slowly pulled her to him. She knew he was giving her a chance to step away, but she didn't want to.

She wanted this to happen.

His deep chocolate eyes came close. Closer.

She welcomed his kiss. It started soft, deepened to affection and tenderness, and then burst into ripe passion.

Yes! She craved this. Craved him.

Michael took her hand and led her to his bedroom, closing and locking the door behind him, where he stopped suddenly.

"What?" Samantha whispered, sensing a cooling in him, a hesitation.

"I—"

"Tell me what's wrong."

"I have this feeling…this— I have to tell you something. It's embarrassing."

"What is it? Whatever it is we can get through it together. Is it erectile dysfunction?"

"*What?* God, no!" Michael laughed shakily and raked his fingers through his thick hair.

"I started dating Lillian when I was sixteen," he said.

Samantha waited, not sure where this was going.

"We were always together after that and got married when we were twenty."

When Samantha still didn't respond, he burst out with, "I've only been with one woman."

Samantha breathed a huge sigh. "Is that what's bothering you? I've only been with three men. I had a boyfriend in high school and got married at twenty. Since Kevin left, there's only been— Never mind. I'm not talking about him."

"Really? But look at you. Men must be all over you."

She hardened. She hated the assumptions men made about her appearance. Sure, she looked like a Vegas showgirl, but she wasn't one.

"Because of the way I look, men think I'm some kind of sex goddess. I'm a woman, okay? Just a normal woman."

Michael leaned back against the closed door.

"I am not my body," she said. "I'm not my face. I have depth and a brain and feelings."

He tucked his fingers into his pockets.

"I like sex, but no more than the average woman. My sex drive is healthy, but I'm not sex driven. Do you understand the difference?"

"Yeah, I get it." He scrubbed the back of his neck. "To tell you the truth, it's a relief. I worried about having to be some kind of great stud for you."

His vulnerability and honesty charmed her.

"You don't have to be a stud. You just have to be you. Let's just be a man and a woman who care for each other and want to please each other."

He smiled, his relief blossoming like a tidal wave across his face. "That should do the trick."

"Have we dealt with all of your insecurities, Moreno? Can we make love now?"

He grinned and reached for her.

Passion blossomed instantly.

Moments later, their clothes were off and Samantha was holding Michael's spectacular, work-hardened body against hers. It felt like the most beautiful thing on earth.

He opened the drawer of the bedside table and fumbled out a condom.

"Do you always have condoms ready and waiting for women to land here in snowstorms?"

Michael sobered. "No. Lillian and I started using them after she was diagnosed so her body wouldn't have to deal with a pregnancy."

"Oh." She kissed him with sweetness and depth she didn't remember ever feeling for a man before. She loved him. She loved his character and his tenderness and his respect for all creatures.

She tried to put on the condom for him, but her hands fumbled.

"I want you so badly." Her voice was shaky. Between the two of them, they got it on and he entered her with the eagerness of a man in the worst bout of lust.

Samantha laughed and breathed a hearty sigh.

"Oh, Michael," she whispered. "You feel so good."

Her hands roamed his back. She hadn't realized until this moment that she'd been longing to touch him almost from the day she'd arrived.

His massive, warm shoulders and biceps, his smooth skin beneath her hands, came alive.

She loved how big and solid he was. Beneath him, she felt grounded at last, a part of life in a more secure way than she ever had.

This man… This man made her reach for the stars.

Together they fought their climaxes to make their lovemaking last, but desire defeated them and it was over too soon.

They lay spent, lazily tracing circles on each other's bodies. Samantha had never felt so content, so filled with love. Where had this come from?

Long minutes later, he rolled out of bed, stepped into his jeans and left the room. He returned smelling of soap and carrying a warm damp washcloth for her.

He picked up the sweat suit she slept in every night and handed it to her.

"I know you need this. I grew up in a cold house, not in a hot house like you city slickers," Michael joked.

"Quit with the generalities, okay?" Sammy smacked his chest. "We had no money when we were young. There were plenty of times when all the utilities were cut off."

She shrugged into the clothes he'd handed her.

"I slept many a night without heat, macho man."

Michael finished putting on his sweatpants

and long-sleeved T-shirt. “Macho man? I’ll show you—”

Sammy cut him off. “You already did.” She giggled.

Michael grinned, picked her up and tossed her onto the bed. She giggled again.

He crawled into bed beside her and pulled her close, hauling up the bedclothes to cover both of them.

Their clothes didn’t last long. Soon enough, hands explored under them and then threw them off and tossed them to the floor.

It took a while to come back down to earth, but she did it in Michael’s arms and she’d never felt anything so good.

In time, they got dressed again and spooned.

With Michael, Sammy found the security and contentment that had been missing from her life until now.

She kissed his palm and laid it on her stomach.

“Michael,” she whispered. Just his name. That was enough.

“Sammy.” He kissed her cheek.

It had been a long time since she’d been so sated…and so happy.

Michael awoke to a wild animal pummeling his chest.

“Wha—?”

"Pig! Leave my mom alone." Jason lay half across him, hitting him. "I thought you were okay, but you're just like all the other men."

Damn! He'd forgotten to lock the door after he'd gone to the washroom. Michael cursed his carelessness.

Beside him, Sammy cried out.

Jason got in a few good whacks at Michael's face before Michael managed to trap the boy's fists in one of his own.

He heaved himself up out of bed and wrapped his arm around the struggling child.

Lit by the meager winter moonlight struggling through the window, the boy's ravaged expression saddened Michael. Tears streamed down Jason's cheeks. Poor kid. The betrayal coursing through his thin body thundered through Michael.

"It's not what you think." Michael kept his voice low and steady. He caught a glimpse of Sammy's shattered expression.

She reached for her son, but Michael shook his head. "Leave him to me. You've meddled in my life, now it's my turn to meddle in yours. He needs a heart-to-heart with a man, not with his mother. Stay here."

He knew she wouldn't, but Michael wanted to protect her in case her son started spewing nonsense that might hurt his mom.

Jason kicked and yelled.

Michael squeezed him, aware of his own strength and of the boy's vulnerability. He didn't want to hurt him, only control him before he hurt himself.

"Hush," he said. "Don't wake the little kids."

"They should wake up," Jason cried, but Michael noted he modulated his voice. Even in this desperate situation, the kid was conscious of the need to take care of the younger children. "They should see the kind of man you really are." Jason did a good job of bruising Michael's shins with his sharp heels. "You lied to us. You fooled us. I trusted you."

His voice cracked and Michael's heart broke for the boy.

"No, I didn't fool you." He carried him down the long hallway to the living room, making sure the bedrooms were silent as they passed. All was quiet except for the hellion in his arms, whom he plunked down onto the sofa.

When Jason made a move to run, Michael corralled him and put him back, this time with a hand around his wrists and an arm across his thighs to immobilize those deadly heels.

With his foot, Michael snagged the coffee table, pulled it close and sat down facing Jason.

Jason wriggled.

Quietly, Michael said, "I love her."

It had come out of nowhere, this second love in his life. He'd resisted and resisted, but could no longer deny what had happened.

Jason struggled on.

Michael raised his voice. "Listen to me. I love your mother."

He meant it. It had sneaked up on him. In a ridiculously short time, he'd fallen like a ton of bricks, head over heels and every other cliché in the book.

Jason had stopped moving and stared at him, that wry twist of his lips mocking Michael.

"That's what all the men say, but they never mean it. My dad didn't mean it. Greg didn't mean it. I hated how he looked at Mom. He was a creep."

Michael hated that cynical smile. A boy Jason's age shouldn't have a care in the world, shouldn't know about men lying to his mother, but Michael figured he'd probably been looking out for his mom since the second his father farted off to the Himalayas to *find himself.* Just before falling asleep, Samantha had shared a few secrets with him.

Some men had no sense of responsibility. This boy was working overtime to make up for his father's lack.

"I miss my dad."

The stark grief in Jason's voice broke Michael's heart.

"I know you do. I don't blame you." Unfortunately, it was too soon to start talking about becoming the new father in Jason's life.

"I'm more responsible than he was. I plan to love your mom forever."

"You don't mean it." In the kid's tone, Michael heard both disbelief and hope.

Since Jason was no longer struggling, Michael released him.

Jason sat back and crossed his arms, mulish and righteous, not willing to give in too easily. This child had had his dreams shattered countless times already.

"I do mean it," Michael stressed. "I know it's hard for you to believe. It's been fast, I admit that, but it's true."

Michael wasn't used to talking or sharing. He held things in, but Jason deserved nothing less than the truth.

"When your mom walks into a room, she lights it up," Michael tried to explain. "She's like a ray of sunshine."

"I know, right? She's a happy person. But

men don't see that." Still agitated, Jason knocked his heels against the sofa. "Men see the way she looks. Her blond hair. Her amazing pretty face. Her big…you know…and they don't see anything else. It was like that in Las Vegas all the time 'cause they thought she was one of the showgirls."

"Men are shallow." Michael nodded. Hard to fight the truth.

"Yeah, like that creep Greg. He didn't love Mom. He only wanted to…you know."

Michael would have to ask Sammy about Greg. "There's more to her than that."

Jason stopped his agitated knocking. "Yeah. She doesn't light up rooms 'cause she's pretty, but 'cause of all the goodness inside that leaks out of her."

Pure, simple beauty out of the mouth of a babe.

The goodness inside that leaks out of her.

That was exactly right.

Jason might be only nine years old, but he was wise beyond his years. He was a hell of a lot older than he should be. It was time for him to be a kid again.

A soft sound alerted Michael to Sammy's presence. She stood in the living room doorway quietly crying, her inner goodness leaking out of her.

He returned his attention to Jason. "You know what I see when I look at you?"

Jason shook his head, eyes too big in his young face.

"I see the man you're going to be, and it's a good one. Someday you are going to be even more strong and wise and trustworthy than you are today."

The kid had it all already going on in spades.

"But right now," Michael went on, "you need to just be a kid."

"I can't," Jason wailed, face crumpling, falling apart again. "Who'll take care of my mom?"

Michael moved from the coffee table to sit on the sofa, taking Jason onto his lap as though he were as small as Lily. Jason didn't resist.

Michael cradled his head against his shoulder, infusing Jason with all the security his strong arms could offer.

As a testament to how upset Jason was, he didn't object to being held like a toddler.

When Jason had cried himself out, Michael said, "You never have to worry about your mom again. From now on, I'll take care of her."

A quiet *humph* emanated from the woman

hiding in the doorway. Michael held back a laugh. He'd get an earful about that later.

Yes, she could take care of herself, he knew that, but he wanted to be the one she turned to in times of need. He wanted his shoulder to be the one she leaned on.

One thing was certain. He'd only just found Samantha. No way was he ever letting her walk out of his life again.

"I'm really tired," Jason murmured, sounding waterlogged.

"I bet you are. A good cry takes a lot out of a man."

"Yeah." He pulled away from Michael's chest. "Don't tell my mom I cried, okay? I don't want her to worry."

Michael heard soft scurrying down the hallway as Samantha returned to his room.

"I won't tell her." An easy promise to keep.

"I'm going back to bed." Jason climbed from his lap and stood up, cheeks tinged pink.

Time to help the boy save face. Michael stood, too. "Thanks for doing a great job of taking care of your mom. I'm proud of you."

He stuck out his hand.

Jason stared, then shook it.

"I'll take over from here," Michael assured him.

"'Kay. Thanks, Michael." Jason walked

back to his bedroom looking about fifty pounds lighter.

Michael returned to his room and took Sammy into his arms.

"It's all good," he said. "Jason is fine."

"I heard everything you said. Did you mean it?"

"Every word of it."

"Oh. I think I'm going to cry again." She burrowed against him.

"You did a great job with Jason. He's an amazing kid."

"Yeah, he is, isn't he?" Her voice sounded as watery as her son's had.

"You're well grounded. You have common sense. You haven't let your beauty go to your head. Your parents did a good job, too."

"My parents had nothing to do with it." Michael reeled away from the rancor in her voice. If distaste could be made visible, she'd done so with her curled lips and tight fists.

"It was all Travis," she said, voice softened. "He's the one who raised me. He did a damned good job of it."

He touched her hair, brushing it back from her face. "He sure did."

He urged her into bed and pulled her against him.

"I love you, too," she whispered.

Michael Moreno fell asleep with a smile on his face.

Chapter 13

Christmas-in-February morning arrived early with Lily jumping onto Samantha's bed. Sammy awoke to a sharp elbow to her ribs and a loud, "Oomph."

"Sammy, happy Christmas-in-February morning! Can we start now?"

Samantha cast a bleary eye toward the other side of the bed. Michael must have decided to move back to the sofa. Wise man. "It isn't even light out yet. For Pete's sake, what time is it?"

Lily shrugged. "I don't know. I can't tell time, Sammy. I'm too young."

"We'll have to fix that pronto," Samantha grumbled. She picked up her watch.

"Five fifteen?" She groaned and collapsed against her pillow. "I need my sleeeeep."

Lily giggled.

Sammy distracted her with whispered talk for a while but Lily said, "Sammy, I'm tired of waiting."

Samantha checked the time again. "Five thirty." She wasn't sure how much longer she could hold Lily off.

"Tell you what," she said. "I'll get one present and bring it back for you to open in here. Okay?"

Lily bounded off the bed, but Samantha snagged the back of her pajama top and pulled her back.

"You stay here." The last thing she wanted was for Lily to see the stockings before the rest of the family was up.

"Here's the deal," she said. "You wait for me here and I will bring you back one present to open. If you won't stay here, you don't get to open gifts early. Got it?"

Lily nodded vigorously.

Samantha rolled out of bed and shoved her feet into the slippers she'd crocheted with remnants from the yarn she'd used for the boys' mittens.

She tiptoed down the dark hallway and strategized about gift opening. Which would

Lily be most excited about? Samantha would save that for last. Definitely her clothes. Lily would be thrilled with her Christmas-in-February outfit.

In the end, Samantha chose one of Puff's outfits for Lily to open early.

Michael whispered, "What's up?"

"Lily's awake. I'm trying to appease her with one present."

"Turn on the tree lights." His deep voice rumbled across the room. He lay on his back with his hands under his head. She wanted nothing more than to crawl under the old quilt with him.

She turned on the Christmas tree lights and sighed. Beautiful. The tree glowed in the darkness, festive and pretty, dispelling the gloom.

She picked up one of Puff's gifts and walked softly back to the hallway. There, leaning as far out of her bedroom as she could, stood Lily.

When Lily tried to get a better look at the sliver of living room at the end of the hallway, she toppled over onto her side and let out a wail.

Samantha ran to her and gathered her up, muffling her crying with her shoulder.

"Shh." She hustled into the bedroom and

closed the door before the boys woke. She'd been hoping that maybe Lily could be persuaded to stay in bed for another hour or two after opening her gift.

Not likely, but a tired woman could always dream.

She sat on her bed with Lily in her lap. "Where are you hurt?"

"Nothing hurts, Sammy."

Samantha frowned. "Then why are you crying?"

"I want my present."

"You'll get it. Why do you think you won't?"

"I fell out into the hallway. My toe was still in the room, but I lost my balance. I didn't leave the room on purpose."

"I know that, honey. Now stop the waterworks. Here's your gift."

Lily's tears shut off pretty darn quickly and she reached for the brightly decorated package.

Tearing at the paper that had taken them so long to produce—plain newsprint paper decorated with stars made from potatoes and a gold stamp pad—Lily made quick work of opening it.

"It's little tiny clothes. Look! Pretty clothes!"

"Yes, I know. I made them."

Lily held the skirt against her body. "It's too small, Sammy."

"It's not for you, silly. Think. Who would wear a skirt that small?"

Lily's face lit up. "Puff!"

She jumped off the bed, retrieved the doll from the floor and climbed back up beside Samantha. She started tearing off Puff's old pants so roughly Sammy feared they would tear.

"Let me. Then you can put the skirt on."

She undressed the doll, then Lily took over and managed to get the skirt on. "Sammy, she looks so pretty."

She didn't. Puff looked old and ragged, but the skirt helped considerably. Lily held her with love and that was all that mattered.

Samantha lay down while Lily talked to her doll. Eventually, the child lay down beside Sammy and the two of them dozed.

An hour and a half later, Samantha awoke in a better mood.

She heard whispers in the hallway. The boys. They couldn't have been too quiet because she heard them through the closed door. So...whispers that were designed to awaken her.

She grinned.

She should make them suffer and lie here for another half hour, but she didn't have it in her.

For the second time that morning, she slipped out of bed, not worrying about waking Lily. Christmas-in-February morning was officially about to begin.

She opened the door and found three eager boys standing in their pajamas. Just then the back door opened and Michael stepped in, bringing with him the early-morning chill of a new winter day.

Memories of last night's intimacy shimmered between them like a heat wave. He looked too serious.

"Merry Christmas in February!" Samantha declared and the boys erupted in laughter and shouting.

"Come on," she said. "Let's do Christmas in our pajamas."

When she turned to Michael, she forced herself to sound normal. "How are the animals?"

"Good. Sound." His cheeks flushed and he continued, "They got extra feed this morning for Christmas."

Oh, my. Was he getting into the spirit of the day?

"Christmas in February," Lily corrected, rubbing her eyes. "Daddy, look at Puff!"

She launched herself at her father just as he was getting out of his shearling coat. He caught her with one arm and hauled her against his chest.

"I can't look at Puff."

"Why not, Daddy?"

"I'm too busy looking at my beautiful daughter!" He blew a raspberry on her neck and she giggled.

When he finished, Lily said, "Daddy, you have to look at Puff. She's different this morning."

Michael took the doll from her and raised his brows exaggeratedly. "She's got a new skirt! How did that happen? Did *some*body start Christmas in February early?"

A small hand tugged on Samantha's arm. Mick, expression crestfallen, watched her with eyes full of accusation. "How come Lily got to open a present before us?"

"Because she woke me at *five fifteen* and wouldn't let me *sleep*. I would have done *anything* to get more sleep. I bribed her with a present." She brushed an errant lock of hair from Mick's eyes. "Someday when you're a parent, you will learn the true value and *necessity* of bribery."

Mick hunched his shoulders. She'd noticed he liked it when she touched him with motherly affection. "Can we open ours now?"

"You bet. Everyone into the living room and Michael will distribute gifts."

Everyone piled into the room while Samantha started the fire and Michael turned on the coffeepot.

He entered the room and nodded his approval of her fire. "You're getting good at that."

"Thanks. I'll be sad when spring is here and we won't need a fire anymore." Samantha could have bitten her tongue. She wouldn't be *here* in the spring, so what difference would it make? Would she?

He hesitated, as though he didn't know how to broach the subject, either. Fortunately, the children hadn't noticed. They were too busy ogling the presents under the tree.

Michael clapped his hands and they startled. "Everyone away from the tree. Christmas-in-February presents are under my jurisdiction. I get to hand them out."

Samantha could have hugged him. Maybe the day would work out, after all. "Everyone onto the sofa."

The boys scrambled to get there first while

Michael studied the name tags on the packages under the tree.

"Stockings first," she murmured.

Michael made a U-turn and lifted full stockings from the mantel, handing them out to each child.

"Looks like Santa found the house all right, even in February."

Lily and Mick, who'd been too young to remember the stockings their mother had put up for them, handled these with reverence.

Colt said, "Mom, Santa even gave one to me and Jason. We already got ours at December Christmas."

Jason caught her eye and smiled. He hadn't believed in Santa for a few years, but she knew he would play along for the sake of the younger children.

Samantha winked at him. "I guess Santa didn't want you to feel left out."

"Go ahead, kids." Michael seemed excited. "Open them."

They poked and oohed and poured the contents out onto their laps, cheap trinkets, chocolate and candy scattering everywhere.

Michael poured coffee for himself and Samantha, doctoring hers perfectly. Of all of the things he'd done since her arrival, this touched her the most, the thoughtfulness of the gesture, this sharing of small intimacies.

It was all so blessedly normal, but it had never been part of her life, not with her parents and not with her husband.

Michael stood across the room sipping his coffee and smiling down at the children.

Samantha's eyes watered. Shaken and shattered by the simplicity but utter perfection of the moment, she tried to sip her coffee, but her hand shook.

She set it down on the coffee table.

Mick saved her from making a fool of herself by crying when he shouted, "When can we open all of those?"

He pointed to the presents under the tree.

"Load all of your stocking stuffers back into your stockings and put them on your beds." Samantha stood and directed like a drill sergeant. "There's enough mess in here already. Let's clear it up so nothing gets thrown out by mistake."

While the children did as they were told, she got the recycle box from the back porch and set it up at the far end of the sofa.

Michael handed out the smaller packages for the boys. "Lily, you got a present already this morning, so let the boys open their first ones now."

Lily sidled close to Jason to watch him open his gift. Like the very patient older brother he'd grown to be, he let her get in the way.

The boys liked their colorful new mittens. They said all the appropriate thank-yous, but she and Michael knew they were waiting for the main-event presents, the bigger boxes. She'd caught the younger boys shaking them a couple of times already.

Lily got her other small gift next. She squealed when she opened the new top and jacket for Puff. She wanted everyone to wait while she dressed her doll, but Michael put his foot down.

"We can't make the boys wait, Lily. Besides, don't you want your big present?"

"Yes!" She dropped Puff, who stared wide-eyed from the floor as though in betrayal.

Samantha picked up the doll and her new clothing and set them on the coffee table.

Lily tore at the paper and her new skirt spilled out. She held it up by a corner of the hem. "What is it, Sammy?"

"It's a new skirt for you to wear today." She held it up properly by the waist.

Lily clapped and jumped to her feet. "Look at the sparkly leaves. Put it on me."

"What's the magic word?"

"*Please*, Sammy, put it on me."

Samantha pulled it up over her pajama bottoms and Lily twirled around. At the child's squeals, Sammy was glad she'd made such a large circumference at the hem.

"What's this?" Lily asked when her father handed her a second package.

"The other half of your present."

She opened it and clutched the white eyelet top to her chest. "What is it?"

Her voice quivered with excitement. Samantha couldn't hold her back.

"It's a top to match the skirt." She took off Lily's pajamas and re-dressed her in the long-sleeve top and gilded skirt.

"Look at me!" Lily squealed. "My clothes are pretty."

By comparison, Michael's voice was lower than normal. "Lily, Sammy made those clothes for you."

Lily stared openmouthed. "She maded them all by herself?"

"Yep," Michael answered.

Lily threw her arms around Samantha's neck. "I *love* them, Sammy. You did good."

Every minute spent working late at night, every single moment of sleep lost, was worth it for this one heartfelt hug.

Samantha cleared her throat, but her voice

was still husky. "We should give the boys their presents now."

Mick and Colt loved their Meccano sets. "Hey, look," Mick shouted. "We can make a tractor."

"Later," Samantha said. "Keep the boxes closed until we clean up, and we're going to eat first."

Jason's reaction to his jigsaw puzzle was more subdued, but he was no less excited.

"That looks like Rascal." He pointed to the same horse Michael had noticed.

The gift Jason and Lily had chosen for her was a small figurine of a rabbit with four baby rabbits at her feet.

Four. Four babies. Four children. Oh, if only this fairy tale could come true.

She cleared her throat. "Now your turn," she told Michael. "The last two are yours."

Michael opened his first gift, again with flushed cheeks. He really didn't like attention.

When he saw the ruler, he grinned. "Was this Lily's idea?"

Samantha nodded.

Lily said, "I'll show you how to open it, Daddy."

His eyes met Samantha's because they both knew it had been Michael who had first shown Lily how to do it in the store.

"Thank you, Lily, for your thoughtful gift."

Michael flushed even more deeply when he realized the second gift was a hat. He tried it on. "It fits."

He studied Samantha so intensely she felt her own cheeks warm. "Do you like it?"

"Yeah. A lot. You made it?"

She nodded.

He nodded.

She nodded again. For a moment, she felt as though she were hovering like a tiny creature suspended in amber, the world around her golden and wondrous.

Jason broke the spell by taking Michael's hand and dragging him out of the room.

Samantha tidied up, finding every scrap of paper and depositing it into the recycle bin.

While the children chattered and looked at their new toys—and Jason and Michael were who-knows-where—Samantha took food out of the fridge, all of the breakfast items they would cook over the fire.

It would be a Christmas-in-February Day camping breakfast.

Jason showed up behind her and took her hand, gently urging her out of the kitchen.

"What is it? I have to get breakfast ready."

"You need to come into the living room, Mom."

What was going on? From Jason's quietly pleased expression, she figured it was something good.

Samantha allowed him to drag her into the room where all of the children sat on the sofa without making a peep. Michael stood behind the sofa, watching her, his expression carefully neutral. If she didn't know better, she would think he was nervous.

In front of the armchair was a large box shape covered with an afghan. The armchair itself was empty.

Jason led her over and she sat.

"This is for you, Mom. Michael made it."

Her gaze shot to the man. "Michael made me something?"

Michael shifted on his feet, not quite meeting her eye, but a smile hovered on his lips.

"Merry Christmas in February," he said, voice gruff. "Open it."

Opening it was as simple as lifting off the afghan. Underneath was a small wooden chest about three feet long by two deep and two high. She lifted the lid, closed her eyes and inhaled. The scent of cedar soothed her.

When she opened her eyes, she found Michael watching her, a mixture of pride and uncertainty on his face. He hadn't even wanted Christmas and yet he'd made her a gift, but then she'd learned that Michael cared for the people around him.

"How—? When—?"

He shrugged. "In the stables. In the evenings. Early in the mornings."

She offered him a heartfelt, "Thank you." She couldn't possibly infuse more gratitude into her voice.

Because she couldn't contain the emotions threatening to spill out of her, she turned to her son.

"Did you help?"

"Michael taught me stuff, Mom. He let me use tools."

She returned her attention to Michael. "Thank you, for everything."

He understood what she didn't say. *Thank you for teaching my son.*

To her son, she said, "We'll talk later." She wanted to hear every detail, every little bit of his contribution. What had Michael taught him? She couldn't wait to learn.

She set about making breakfast on the fire, aware of every movement Michael made and of every word he spoke.

Chapter 14

Samantha squealed like Lily when she heard her brother's truck turn onto the driveway.

Travis was coming for dinner, with Rachel and her two children, one an infant.

When Travis stepped into the house with the baby in his arms and a smile on his face, he looked whole in a way she'd never seen before.

Rachel and the little girl standing beside him belonged there.

Samantha finally understood without reservation that he'd made the right choice in moving here.

Rodeo, Montana, made complete and utter sense for Travis Read.

Michael stepped forward and took the baby from Travis so he could remove his outerwear and, Samantha suspected, so she could hug him.

The baby stared at Michael with solemn eyes, but didn't shy away.

"Hey, kid," he said and Samantha laughed. "You're a silver-tongued devil, Michael. You've charmed her."

After hugging Travis, Samantha also hugged Rachel.

"There's a girl here!" Lily pointed from the doorway of the living room.

After introductions were made—the child's name was Victoria, Tori for short—and their coats had been hung up, Lily pointed to the new clothes she wore.

"Sammy maded them. Aren't they pretty?"

"As pretty as can be," Travis said with a glint in his eye. "Don't you make a beautiful Christmas tablecloth?"

"Travis, cut it out!" Samantha laughed. "Save me from bratty older brothers."

To Tori, Lily said, "Come see my doll's new clothes. Sammy maded them, too."

They congregated in the living room.

Michael seemed to have relaxed into having company in his house after so many years of being out of the habit. He rose to the occasion and Sammy couldn't have been more proud of him.

They ate the dinner that Samantha and Michael had made together, crowded around the harvest table in the kitchen.

Never in Sammy's life had she felt part of a family, especially not one so loving and full of affection.

She proposed a toast. The adults raised their wineglasses and the children their juice and water.

"To each and every one of you wonderful people," Samantha said, "who have brought joy to my life."

"Here's to Christmas in February," Michael said quietly, his eyes on Samantha. She warmed beneath his gentle regard.

"Hear, hear," the adults murmured and drank.

"Hear! Hear!" Mick shouted.

Michael sighed. "Hearing aids, Mick."

The child laughed and ran to his room.

Michael found he eased back into the role of host as though it hadn't been more than three years since he'd last played it.

Of all of the things Samantha had done for him, this might be the best. She'd not only brought laughter to his family, but now she also shared her entire family with him.

At six that evening, just before they served dessert, someone knocked on the front door.

Surprised, Michael went to answer. He opened the door.

Damn. It only needed this.

Karen Enright stood on his veranda, her expression equal parts angry and hopeful.

From the kitchen came the sounds of laughter and general merrymaking that had begun early this morning for Christmas in February.

"What's going on, Michael?" she asked.

He tried to see it from her side.

For three years, this house had been a fortress of darkness. Karen had been free to come and go in that last year of Lillian's life. She'd been a godsend, had cared for the children so he could get his chores done, and had helped at times to nurse Lillian so she could stay home.

He'd never asked for her help. It had been freely offered, and yet Michael had felt burdened by the weight of her generosity.

Toward the end, all his wife had asked of him was to die at home.

Karen had helped to make that possible. And how had he repaid her? By pushing her away after Lillian's death. Karen had been a too-visible reminder that Lillian was gone.

As he had with all the other women who'd tried to encroach on the suddenly single man in town, he'd rebuffed her.

While the other women had faded away after the casseroles had been eaten and their dishes returned, Karen hadn't given up. She'd been the one to keep in touch.

And then, she'd been the one pursuing him.

He'd cut himself off from most people, but especially from her.

He couldn't give her what she needed. He wished he could.

In his defense, he'd always been honest with her.

Her fingers twisted the handles of her purse when he was silent so long. Again she asked, "What's going on, Michael?"

How could he explain that none of this had been his idea, that he'd been dragged kicking and screaming into it, but now that Christmas in February was here, it felt right?

"You haven't been returning my calls." Karen stepped into the hallway. He had no choice but to let her in. "I heard rumors in town."

He cleared his throat. "About what?"

"That you have a woman here."

"It's not the way you think."

"Then it's true?" She tried to see around him, but he didn't want her to, yet another complication in a life that had become nothing *but* complications.

He cursed that he couldn't change the truth, that he couldn't love Karen.

"Let me explain." He crossed his arms, as though he could ward off this entire conversation. As though he could ward off *her*. But that was unfair.

He owed Karen a lot. Not his life or his love or any commitment from him, but she had earned his gratitude and compassion. "Her car broke down the night of the storm."

"The night I was so worried you told me not to come over, you already had a woman here?"

"Not like that! I didn't want her here, either, but she and those two boys would have died if they'd stayed in the car."

"So you took them in?" She rested her fingers on his arm. "I admire your generosity, but why is she still here? That is her I hear, right? In your kitchen? The storm was eleven or twelve days ago."

"I know, but the snow wasn't cleared and the children like her, and we didn't have Christmas, and..." He wasn't making sense. He barely knew how to make sense of it himself.

This situation, these events, had flattened him. No, he didn't have control over his life right now, and he wasn't sure he wanted it.

He heard Lily talking, her voice high and sweet and animated. She was happy. He was happy.

A stranger had stepped into his dark home out of a howling snowstorm and had worked her magic, filling his house with light and noise and messy days and peaceful nights.

Above all, she had filled his house with joy.

Michael sighed loudly, and Karen's demeanor changed. She knew without him saying so that whatever hopes she'd cherished had been dashed.

Samantha Read had brought joy into his home, and he planned to grasp it with both hands and never let go.

She belonged here.

Her boys belonged here.

Karen turned to go, but he touched her arm. He couldn't watch her walk out of here so unhappy when she had done so much for him and his family.

No, he didn't love her, but now that he was

free of her expectations, he realized how much affection he felt. She had a heart of gold.

"Would you—? Do you think...?" She was hurting and he didn't like that, but was it right to invite her in to share the enjoyment everyone else was having in his home?

Would she want it? Or would it hurt her more?

God, he didn't know. He was a simple rancher, not a psychiatrist.

All he knew was that it felt right to share with Karen, even if only something as mundane as a slice of pie and a cup of coffee.

"You wouldn't want to join us, would you?" Michael asked. "The kids would love to see you. And I would like you to stay."

She seemed to fight within herself and settled on a nod. She didn't look happy. Maybe she was joining them out of curiosity. Maybe she just wanted to meet the woman who was becoming part of his life.

"Let me take your coat." He hung it on a hook and led her into the kitchen.

"Hey, everyone, look who's here."

Lily squealed, "Karen!" and launched herself at her. The ice was broken. Karen lifted Lily into her arms and tousled Mick's hair.

He grinned at her. "Hi, Aunt Karen."

"Karen." Michael took her elbow and drew her close to the table. "You know Rachel."

Rachel gave a small wave and smiled. "Nadine said you offered to help in the summer at the fair. I appreciate it. We'll probably work you to exhaustion."

Rachel laughed and Karen responded with a soft smile. "I love what you women are doing. It will be nice to have the excitement of the fair and rodeo back in town."

If Karen's voice wasn't quite steady who could blame her? Michael's house had been quiet and empty for three years and now it was full. Karen had hoped to be the woman to fill it. Her hopes had been dashed.

Only now, when it was too late, did he realize how much there was to admire about her, like the grace she was displaying now.

He left the room to get another chair. "We'll squeeze you in here between Mick and Lily."

"I'd like that," she said.

"Karen, have you met Travis Read?"

"No. I've seen you around town, but we've never met." She shook his hand.

"Beside him are his nephews, Colt and Jason."

Jason stood, walked around the table and shook Karen's hand. Colt grinned and waved.

Michael gestured toward Samantha at the far end of the table.

"This is Samantha, Travis's sister."

Samantha's welcome was warm. "Your timing is impeccable. Would you like dessert? We're just about to cut into a couple of pies."

She stood up. "I'm sorry, I didn't catch your name."

"Karen Enright."

Samantha's smile was brilliant. "What a funny way to meet! I'm your new employee."

Gobsmacked, Michael stared, his gaze shifting between the two. "What are you talking about?"

"I'm going to be starting work for Karen's company next month, once the boys and I are a little more settled."

He remembered her mentioning that she was an accountant, but not that she had a job lined up in town.

Samantha had no idea who Karen was, and what she'd hoped for with Michael. How would it affect her job?

Karen's expression, he noted, was carefully neutral.

She put together a place setting for Karen and then said, "Michael, can you get a coffee?"

Karen put her hand over her cup before he could pour. "Only if it's decaf."

"It is," Samantha said. "I'd be up all night if it wasn't. Since this morning started just after five, I'm exhausted. I need my beauty sleep."

"No, you don't."

Everyone turned to stare at Karen. Michael held his breath. What did she mean? Was she about to get catty or biting?

"You are quite stunning already." Karen's voice was clean and true, uncolored by sarcasm. "I don't think I've ever seen a more beautiful woman."

Samantha blushed. "I don't know what to say to that. It's not as though it's a great accomplishment. I've never done anything to earn it." She laughed and pointed to her sons. "My biggest accomplishment was having these two rascals. That's about it."

"Hey, sis," Travis said. "Don't sell yourself short. What you did to Manny d'Onofrio took real courage. You're a hero."

"Manny who?" Michael asked. "What are you talking about?"

"Manny was my old boss in Vegas. I caught him embezzling from the hotel I worked for and called the FBI."

"She testified against him at his trial." Travis took up the story. "He was an angry, powerful man who promised to hunt her down and ki—" He glanced at the children. "Find her. So she and the kids took her maiden name and hid out in San Francisco."

"That's why Travis bought this house in Rodeo. Because it's remote."

"Manny wrote to Sammy before Christmas. He found religion."

"Yes," Sammy continued. The two of them made a great tag team. "He's come to a new understanding of life. He's old. He won't live long. He'll spend the rest of his life in jail."

She shrugged. "I guess he took stock and decided repentance was better than revenge."

"Thank goodness," Travis said. "I'm glad Sammy and the boys are safe."

Travis was right. What Samantha had done had taken courage, but then, wasn't that just her? She'd stood up against Michael's anger to do the right things for his children, and for him.

The night ended early, with Karen saying little before she left. At the door, Michael hugged her and said, "You are welcome in my home anytime, Karen."

He found he meant it.

With hugs all around, Travis, Rachel and the two girls left.

Samantha and Michael put the children to bed, then stared at each other in the sudden silence.

"What now?" Samantha looked as uncertain as he'd ever seen her.

"Now we turn in, too."

"That's not what I meant. I wasn't talking about just tonight."

"I know." He drew her against his chest, his big hand on her soft hair. "I once thought that lightning couldn't strike twice. I'd known love with Lillian. How could that possibly happen again? Then you came along."

She leaned away from him to gaze into his eyes.

"Did lightning strike?"

"I've been singed. Scorched. I might never recover."

He didn't have romantic words, but he could be himself. He could lay his heart on the line.

"Will you marry me, Sammy?"

She burst into tears.

"Why do women get weepy when they're happy?" He grasped her arms. "Wait a minute. You are happy, right?"

The wrong answer could break his heart.

"I'm ecstatic, but no, I can't marry you."

She'd sucker punched him. "No?" The word bled out of him along with his hope.

She stepped away from him. "I can't. I want to, but I know that I would start to depend on you too much. I depended on Travis for too long. I have to learn to be independent. To take care of myself."

When he stepped close, she raised her hand. "Please let me finish. I married Kevin too young, and too early in our relationship, because I thought he could provide a home and stability for me. Did you hear that? I said *for* me."

She stood straight, back rigid, as though she needed to get through this quickly. "I shouldn't have expected other people to make my life. It was always my own responsibility. I realize that now."

Michael didn't have a clue what to say. He'd found love, but Sammy was rejecting it. He had no words to help her change her mind.

"Sure, Kevin should have done a better job of providing for his children, but I shouldn't have asked him to put my wishes ahead of his."

"But you're moving into a house your brother bought for you."

"I know. It doesn't sound like it makes

sense, does it? But the original plan was for us to move in and for Travis to eventually move on like he always does."

She chewed on her lip. "I had no intention of just taking the house from him. I planned to pay him back every cent of the down payment over time and take over the mortgage payments, as well. I wouldn't allow him to give it to me."

"What about Rachel and her children? Don't you think Travis will keep the house for himself now?"

"Yes. He's told us it's large enough for all of us, but I don't know..."

"So move in here with me. It's the perfect solution."

She shook her head. "No, Michael. The perfect solution is for me to find a place for my family on my own."

Michael didn't want to ask, but had to. "Do you feel anything for me?"

She closed her eyes and pressed a fist against her chest. "I feel *everything* for you."

"Then give me tonight."

Her eyes flew open. "What?"

"Come to my bed. Make love with me. Give me this last gift."

He reached out his hand. It wasn't even a

fraction of what he wanted, but tonight he needed Sammy. He held his breath.

"Yes." She placed her hand in his and he led her to his bedroom, making sure to lock the door.

Chapter 15

They sat in the living room quietly. The children were absorbed in their own entertainment, the adults in their own thoughts.

In a couple of hours, Travis was coming to pick them up. Sammy's car had been towed, but the mechanic was waiting for a part.

Michael sat on the sofa, gripping Samantha's hand. He'd told her he didn't want her to go. She wouldn't let him convince her to stay.

Her usually sunny mood was strained. She hadn't smiled all morning. She'd never been more miserable in her life, giving up love for…what? Independence? Was she—?

The front door burst open. Everyone startled. Travis wouldn't enter Michael's house forcefully without knocking first. Michael surged to his feet.

"Stay put," he yelled over his shoulder as he hurried out of the room.

Heart pounding, Samantha held her breath when Michael disappeared. Strangely, she heard no sounds in the hallway, no confrontation, no conversation.

Her Spidey Sense went into overdrive.

Michael backed into the living room wordlessly, arms raised.

Manny's top men, Frank and Karl, followed him into the room, holding him at gunpoint.

Sammy's heart sank.

Manny had lied. How could she have been so stupid as to believe him?

She stood up, gesturing with her hand for the children to stay seated.

They disobeyed, clinging to her in wide-eyed fear, except for Jason who stood behind her.

She tried to edge the other three children behind her, too, but they resisted, terrified but also fascinated by the big men and their guns.

Big men, sure, but soft.

Michael, fit and strong and fiercely protective of his children, could have overcome them both easily, except for those paralyzing guns.

She wasn't afraid of the men. She would gladly help Michael take them down. The guns were what scared her. Even if they could disarm the men, a finger could pull a trigger. Terror filled her at the thought of one of the children being hurt.

Frank and Karl had aged in the past couple of years and looked gaunt, haggard, and desperate.

"Why are you here?" Samantha gently urged Lily behind her. Mick stubbornly refused to move, as did Colt. "Manny told me he called off the hunt."

Frank snorted, one of the man's many weird quirks that had never endeared him to her. "Yeah, we heard about that from Manny. He got religion."

Religion might as well have been *syphilis* for all of the disgust in Frank's tone.

"So why are you here?" she repeated.

"We want some of that money you took from Manny."

Her expression flattened. They thought she had Manny's *money*? She was the one who'd turned him in, for God's sake! "Manny didn't give me anything."

"I didn't say *give*, I said *took*." Frank favored his right foot. She remembered his bad knees. He'd been a football player before starting to work for Manny. Over the years his bulk had morphed from muscle to fat.

"I didn't take any money, Frank. Manny was the guilty one. Not me."

"There was a half million the Feds never recovered."

"Talk to Manny about that. I don't have it."

Frank snorted again. Lovely. "You expect me to believe you never skimmed any off the top for yourself before you ratted on the boss?"

Samantha rolled her eyes. The man sounded like a lousy B-movie actor. "If I'd done that, would I have called the FBI?"

"You're smart. You're good with numbers. You woulda found a way."

"I didn't. I guess given the people with whom you associate you're not used to meeting someone honest."

"Not in our line of work." That was Karl speaking, the coarseness of his voice getting worse. He obviously hadn't quit smoking.

"I'm the exception."

"I don't think so." She was back to sparring with Frank. "We got nothin'. No nest egg. No retirement. You need to cough up what you took."

"Do you think that if I had thousands stashed away I'd be here now depending on this rancher?" She spread her arms to encompass the living room. "Why wouldn't I be living it up somewhere in luxury?"

Frank hesitated, casting a glance around the room and noting the same decorations she had when she'd first arrived.

"This ain't your style, no," Frank conceded.

Maybe not, but she'd grown used to it. The old tools and evidence of the ranch's history and heritage couldn't be separated from Michael. They were a deep part of him and they were dear to her.

She could live here. She *wanted* to live here, in this house *exactly* as it stood.

She sensed Jason moving and wanted to stop him, but didn't want to bring the men's attention to her son.

Please, please, please, don't do anything foolish.

"How did you find me? Manny?"

"Not directly, no, but I was there when Vivian told Manny where she'd found you. We asked around town. Heard you'd landed here in a storm."

"You can get back out of here."

Frank scowled and stepped forward, reaching for her, but his bad knee gave out.

Michael dived for him. Karl made a move

to help, but Sammy got to him first, shoving one knuckle against the base of his throat.

She dug the fingernails of her other hand between two of Karl's knuckles. His hand went limp and the gun fell to the floor. She picked it up and, for good measure, kneed him in the groin.

Jason dived for the phone.

A gunshot rang out. They stilled.

Frank fell to the floor, unconscious.

Michael staggered away from him with blood running down his arm.

Samantha lunged for Frank's gun.

"What's wrong with him?" She spun to Michael. "Why are you bleeding?" Her voice rose.

"I called nine-one-one," Jason said, his voice shaking. "They need to know what the address is here."

Michael rattled it off. Jason repeated it into the phone and added, "We need the sheriff and an ambulance."

"I knocked him out. But the gun went off when he fell. He got me."

Samantha cried out. She heard the children sobbing. She knelt on the floor beside Michael, with no clue what to do.

She loved this man. He couldn't possibly

be hurt. “You can’t die,” she sobbed. “I won’t let you.”

His smile looked wan. “I’m not dying. Hurt, though.”

He took in the entire room. “Jason, run out to the stable and get some rope or a harness. Samantha, calm down the children. When Jason comes back, tie up those two.”

He took the gun from Sammy and trained it on Karl.

Samantha took the children to the back playroom. “Stay here, okay? Michael will be fine. I’ll take care of him.”

She grabbed towels from the bathroom, fashioning one into a tourniquet above the wound. She didn’t know first aid, but the blood flow slowed.

Frank moaned. Karl wheezed. Jason ran into the room.

With her older son’s help, Samantha got both men tied up.

They heard sirens coming down the highway, and the children came running from the back room. Samantha knew it was pointless to shoo them out again. They needed to be with her and Michael.

A man she assumed was the sheriff burst into the house.

He introduced himself. “Cole Payette. You are?”

“Samantha Read. Michael Moreno’s been shot.”

“Are the perps Manny’s men?”

Surprised, she asked, “You know about them?”

“Travis warned me.”

Paramedics followed Cole inside. “This way.”

After the sheriff heard the story and Michael had been patched up, the paramedics left.

Sheriff Payette and his deputy hauled Frank and Karl to their feet to herd them to their cruiser.

“Rest up tonight, Michael,” the sheriff told him. “Usually I would need you at the station right away to give your full statement.”

Frank groaned. Payette ignored him. “As the medic said, it’s only a surface wound, but I’ll cut you some slack anyway.”

He scanned everyone’s faces, including the children. “Come in tomorrow to give your statements. I’ll be glad to get this scu—these bad guys into jail.”

With that, he grinned and headed out.

Samantha cleaned up the detritus left behind by the paramedics.

"The carpet will have to be cleaned."

"We'll get a new one," Michael said. Though he looked a little gray, he seemed in fine spirits.

There he went with that *we* business again that she loved so much. She could have lost him. But she couldn't think about it, not now, or she would break down.

"Jason," she said quietly, "would you please take the children into the back room to play? I need a moment with Michael."

"Wait," Michael interjected. "Jason, come here first."

Her son approached. Michael held out his hand and shook Jason's. "I saw you sneaking over to the phone to call for help. Thank you. That's about the bravest thing I've seen. You have more courage than many men I know."

Jason leaned close and whispered, "I was scared."

"But you did it anyway. That's the definition of courage. I'm proud of you."

Jason nodded. His thin throat worked while he swallowed. He said, "I'm proud of you, too, Michael. I want to be like you when I grow up."

With his good arm, Michael hauled her son against his chest and Samantha had to turn away.

They released their holds on each other and Jason led the children to the back of the house.

As soon as they were out of sight, Sammy burrowed against Michael and held him. "I thought I'd lost you."

He held her as if he would never let her go. His grip hurt. She didn't want him to stop.

In time, he set her away so he could look at her.

"That stuff you told me about learning independence and strength?"

She nodded.

"I respect that."

She sensed there was more to come and waited. Michael had taught her that not every silence needed to be filled. He'd taught her to calm down. She liked the feeling.

"But here's the thing," he said. "There are different kinds of strength. I'm good at providing. It's what I was raised to do and what I have talent for. I know it's old-fashioned, but I like it. I do it well."

Michael didn't give speeches. She watched him, waiting for the point.

"You have a different kind of strength I can't begin to match. Jason was right. When you walk into a room all golden and beautiful, your goodness radiates from within. You are full of joy. You spread that joy wherever you go."

He brushed his hand across her hair. "You've brought my children joy. You've brought me back to life. Despite everything that's happened to you, you still smile. If that isn't strength, I don't know what is."

His fingers trailed along her jaw. She shivered. "Can't we combine our strengths and support each other's weaknesses? Can't we make a perfect whole?"

He made such beautiful sense that she nodded. She could no longer see his handsome face through her tears.

"Marry me?"

"Yes!"

"Kids," Michael called, "come here."

When they entered the room, he said, "Sit down, I need to ask y'all something."

Once they had settled, he gestured for Sammy to sit on the sofa beside him.

He squeezed her hand.

"Sammy and I are getting married," he said. "Are you all okay with that?"

After a stunned silence, the kids erupted with joyful hoots and hollers. Nothing had ever felt more perfect or more right for Samantha.

Lily climbed up on her father and asked, “What’s married?”

Michael started to explain about blended families and shared responsibilities. Sammy laughed and interrupted. “It means that Colt, Jason and I are going to live here with you forever. We aren’t ever going to leave. Never, ever again.”

Lily’s little smile spread slowly as comprehension set in.

“It means that I love your father and Mick and you.”

Lily climbed onto her lap and rested her head on Samantha’s shoulder.

“I love you, too, Sammy. And Jason. He’s nice. And Colt, even if he is a boy like Mick. I love Daddy, too. I love you all.”

“And I do, too,” Sammy said, marveling at the steps that had led her to this house, this ranch, on that desperate snowy night—and that this rancher and his children had been here to rescue them from the storm. Michael had rescued her from more than that, filling in all of the empty spaces left by a scarred childhood. And Sammy and her love had rescued him, in turn.

Good fortune had led Samantha Read directly here to Michael Moreno.

"I love all of you." She kissed each and every one of them.

"Oh, no," she said, and everyone stopped talking to look at her and wonder what was wrong, but Jason had a twinkle in his eye. Her son knew her so well.

"I feel a song coming on!"

Jason groaned. "Not disco, Mom."

"Sister Sledge!"

Sammy started to dance even before she started singing, "We are family…"

The children, Jason included, joined her in song and danced around her.

In time, Michael, her big taciturn rancher, broke into a huge grin, took her hand with his good arm, twirled her around until she was dizzy, and joined her in song.

* * * * *

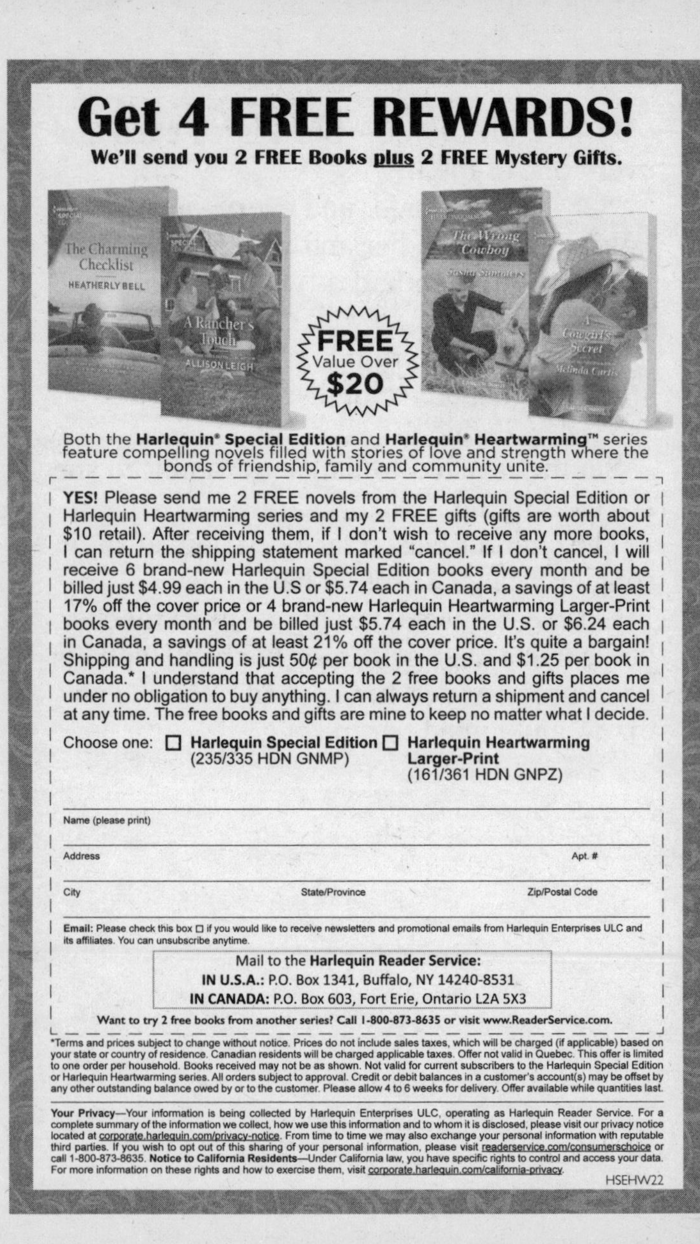

Get 4 FREE REWARDS!
We'll send you 2 FREE Books plus 2 FREE Mystery Gifts.
The Charming Checklist
HEATHERLY BELL
A Rancher's Touch
ALLISON LEIGH
The Wrong Cowboy
A Cowgirl's Secret
Melinda Curtis
FREE
Value Over
$20
Both the Harlequin® Special Edition and Harlequin® Heartwarming™ series feature compelling novels filled with stories of love and strength where the bonds of friendship, family and community unite.
YES! Please send me 2 FREE novels from the Harlequin Special Edition or Harlequin Heartwarming series and my 2 FREE gifts (gifts are worth about $10 retail). After receiving them, if I don't wish to receive any more books, I can return the shipping statement marked "cancel." If I don't cancel, I will receive 6 brand-new Harlequin Special Edition books every month and be billed just $4.99 each in the U.S or $5.74 each in Canada, a savings of at least 17% off the cover price or 4 brand-new Harlequin Heartwarming Larger-Print books every month and be billed just $5.74 each in the U.S. or $6.24 each in Canada, a savings of at least 21% off the cover price. It's quite a bargain! Shipping and handling is just 50¢ per book in the U.S. and $1.25 per book in Canada.* I understand that accepting the 2 free books and gifts places me under no obligation to buy anything. I can always return a shipment and cancel at any time. The free books and gifts are mine to keep no matter what I decide.
Choose one: ☐ Harlequin Special Edition (235/335 HDN GNMP) ☐ Harlequin Heartwarming Larger-Print (161/361 HDN GNPZ)
Name (please print)
Address
Apt. #
City
State/Province
Zip/Postal Code
Email: Please check this box ☐ if you would like to receive newsletters and promotional emails from Harlequin Enterprises ULC and its affiliates. You can unsubscribe anytime.
Mail to the Harlequin Reader Service:
IN U.S.A.: P.O. Box 1341, Buffalo, NY 14240-8531
IN CANADA: P.O. Box 603, Fort Erie, Ontario L2A 5X3
Want to try 2 free books from another series? Call 1-800-873-8635 or visit www.ReaderService.com.
*Terms and prices subject to change without notice. Prices do not include sales taxes, which will be charged (if applicable) based on your state or country of residence. Canadian residents will be charged applicable taxes. Offer not valid in Quebec. This offer is limited to one order per household. Books received may not be as shown. Not valid for current subscribers to the Harlequin Special Edition or Harlequin Heartwarming series. All orders subject to approval. Credit or debit balances in a customer's account(s) may be offset by any other outstanding balance owed by or to the customer. Please allow 4 to 6 weeks for delivery. Offer available while quantities last.
Your Privacy—Your information is being collected by Harlequin Enterprises ULC, operating as Harlequin Reader Service. For a complete summary of the information we collect, how we use this information and to whom it is disclosed, please visit our privacy notice located at corporate.harlequin.com/privacy-notice. From time to time we may also exchange your personal information with reputable third parties. If you wish to opt out of this sharing of your personal information, please visit readerservice.com/consumerschoice or call 1-800-873-8635. Notice to California Residents—Under California law, you have specific rights to control and access your data. For more information on these rights and how to exercise them, visit corporate.harlequin.com/california-privacy.
HSEHW22

Get 4 FREE REWARDS!
We'll send you 2 FREE Books plus 2 FREE Mystery Gifts.
KENTUCKY CRIME RING
JULIE ANNE LINDSEY
TEXAS STALKER
BARB HAN
FREE
Value Over
$20
UNDER THE RANCHER'S PROTECTION
ADDISON FOX
OPERATION WHISTLEBLOWER
JUSTINE DAVIS
Both the Harlequin Intrigue® and Harlequin® Romantic Suspense series feature compelling novels filled with heart-racing action-packed romance that will keep you on the edge of your seat.
YES! Please send me 2 FREE novels from the Harlequin Intrigue or Harlequin Romantic Suspense series and my 2 FREE gifts (gifts are worth about $10 retail). After receiving them, if I don't wish to receive any more books, I can return the shipping statement marked "cancel." If I don't cancel, I will receive 6 brand-new Harlequin Intrigue Larger-Print books every month and be billed just $5.99 each in the U.S. or $6.49 each in Canada, a savings of at least 14% off the cover price or 4 brand-new Harlequin Romantic Suspense books every month and be billed just $4.99 each in the U.S. or $5.74 each in Canada, a savings of at least 13% off the cover price. It's quite a bargain! Shipping and handling is just 50¢ per book in the U.S. and $1.25 per book in Canada.* I understand that accepting the 2 free books and gifts places me under no obligation to buy anything. I can always return a shipment and cancel at any time. The free books and gifts are mine to keep no matter what I decide.
Choose one: ☐ Harlequin Intrigue Larger-Print (199/399 HDN GNXC) ☐ Harlequin Romantic Suspense (240/340 HDN GNMZ)
Name (please print)
Address
Apt. #
City
State/Province
Zip/Postal Code
Email: Please check this box ☐ if you would like to receive newsletters and promotional emails from Harlequin Enterprises ULC and its affiliates. You can unsubscribe anytime.
Mail to the Harlequin Reader Service:
IN U.S.A.: P.O. Box 1341, Buffalo, NY 14240-8531
IN CANADA: P.O. Box 603, Fort Erie, Ontario L2A 5X3
Want to try 2 free books from another series? Call 1-800-873-8635 or visit www.ReaderService.com.
*Terms and prices subject to change without notice. Prices do not include sales taxes, which will be charged (if applicable) based on your state or country of residence. Canadian residents will be charged applicable taxes. Offer not valid in Quebec. This offer is limited to one order per household. Books received may not be as shown. Not valid for current subscribers to the Harlequin Intrigue or Harlequin Romantic Suspense series. All orders subject to approval. Credit or debit balances in a customer's account(s) may be offset by any other outstanding balance owed by or to the customer. Please allow 4 to 6 weeks for delivery. Offer available while quantities last.
Your Privacy—Your information is being collected by Harlequin Enterprises ULC, operating as Harlequin Reader Service. For a complete summary of the information we collect, how we use this information and to whom it is disclosed, please visit our privacy notice located at corporate.harlequin.com/privacy-notice. From time to time we may also exchange your personal information with reputable third parties. If you wish to opt out of this sharing of your personal information, please visit readerservice.com/consumerschoice or call 1-800-873-8635. Notice to California Residents—Under California law, you have specific rights to control and access your data. For more information on these rights and how to exercise them, visit corporate.harlequin.com/california-privacy.
HIHRS22